Shackled Heart

A Novel

By Crystal Joy

Author of
Completely Captivated and *Completely Yours*

Edited by: Daisycakes Creative Services
Cover design by: Lyndsey Lewellen
Interior Design and Formatting by: BB eBooks

Print Edition
ISBN 13: 978-1978174870
ISBN 10:—197817487X

For Mom and Dad, I couldn't ask for better parents. You've believed in me since I was a little girl, writing stories in a notebook. Your love has not only made an impact on me, but Mac and Charlie's story as well.

Table of Contents

Chapter 1

Minimum Security Prison, Iowa

THE GUARD TWISTED the key, unlocked the cell, and shoved the door open. Metal bars rattled to life. "Wake up," he ordered, moving on to unlock the next inmate's cell.

Charlie Grimm glanced at the alarm clock. Not that he needed to check the time. He'd been awake for over two hours already, eyeing the bright red numbers and counting down the minutes.

He rolled off the hard mattress to stand in front of a small closet filled with jeans and plain blue T-shirts. With no other options, he grabbed pants and a shirt, slipping into them without much consideration. Too bad he couldn't wear a suit or something dressier to make him appear less intimidating, less like a prisoner.

Shifting position in the cramped cell, he turned to face the paint-flecked vanity. He reached for a hair tie and pulled his shoulder-length brown hair back into a low ponytail. The Waterman family wouldn't recognize him. He wasn't the clean-cut businessman they'd once known. That man no longer existed.

He expelled a heavy breath and looked at the clock again. Twenty minutes left until the Waterman family arrived, and his parole meeting began. Time couldn't move fast enough. What would the prison staff say about him? Would they bring up his good behavior? The long hours he'd spent working in the wood shop? He hoped his good behavior counted for something. But would it be enough for the Watermans, or would they argue to keep him locked behind bars?

He cracked his knuckles as doubt seeped in like a poisonous gas, killing all hope of freedom. Of course the family would want him in prison. To guard him from making foolish mistakes. To keep him in captivity, forced to remember his reckless crime.

Charlie couldn't blame the Watermans for wanting justice. He wanted it, too. For Ally's sake.

The alarm clock buzzed. Fifteen minutes. Charlie walked out of his cell and stood in the hallway, glancing back at the small, suffocating space. He shuddered. They couldn't make him go back. He needed fresh air, room to breathe. Somehow, he had to convince Ally's family and the prison staff that he was ready for more responsibility and capable of making better decisions. And most of all, he needed to prove that to himself.

As he walked past the cafeteria, a familiar voice carried through the thin walls and out into the hallway. "You're gonna get it, newbie."

Charlie groaned. Not again. He stepped into the cafeteria, eyeing an unfamiliar man crumpled in a fetal position in the corner of the large, crowded room. The new prisoner covered his face while a muscular, stocky man hovered over him. Charlie didn't have to see the man's face to know who the culprit was. A black spider tattoo crept down the man's shaved head, and eight long legs extended down his neck and onto his collarbone.

Spider was up to his old tricks.

Charlie glanced at the clock in the hallway. Twelve minutes. He should walk away and head to his parole meeting. He couldn't afford to be late. Not when his freedom was on the line.

The man on the floor dropped his shaky hands and looked up at Spider with fear in his eyes. "Why are you doing this?"

Spider laughed, his menacing cackle rising above the echoing roar of men's breakfast conversations. "It's your initiation." He kicked the ball of his foot into the man's chest.

The man on the floor moaned and shielded his body with thin, trembling arms.

Charlie took a step back. If he stayed, the guards would assume he was a part of the fight—eliminating any chance of parole. He should leave. Pretend he hadn't seen any of it. The newbie would survive without his help.

But guilt tugged at him, and he couldn't move any farther. If he left without intervening, Spider would surely beat the man to a bloody pulp. With no time to waste, he stepped behind Spider. "Get away from him."

Spider whirled around, his lips curling into a wicked smile. "If it isn't Charlie. Want to help me extend a warm welcome to our newbie?"

"No." Charlie snorted and crossed his arms.

Anger flashed in Spider's eyes. "Leave us alone, then. You wouldn't want to make a scene, would you?"

Charlie's jaw tightened. "I'm not going anywhere."

Spider looked down at the man on the floor. "He reminds me of you. When he walked in yesterday, I thought he was gonna pee his pants. He was scared out of his wits. Just like you. Remember?"

Charlie remembered all right. The other criminals had looked at him like predators stalking their prey. Pumping weights had been a necessity, the key to his survival against men like Spider. "Leave him alone."

"Just because you're jacked now doesn't mean you can boss me around. It's not like you actually know how to fight."

"You sure about that?" If he didn't end this situation soon, he'd be late for his meeting. It was now or never. He raised his hands, clenched his fists, and eyed Spider's stomach—the perfect place to land a punch, and give Spider what he deserved. "If I didn't know any better, I'd say you're scared."

Spider laughed and shifted his body, shooting a punch right into Charlie's eye. Pain seared through his face. He hunched over, cupping his eye.

Spider jumped on top of the newbie, holding him down as he jabbed at the man's face.

"Help me," the newbie pleaded.

Charlie stepped behind Spider, ready to grab him and pull him off the man on the floor.

"Stop." Two guards rushed over to them, pushing Charlie out of the way as they yanked Spider to a standing position. "That's enough, Spider. Follow me," one of the guards ordered.

The other guard tugged the beaten man to his feet and looked at Charlie, frowning. "You better get some ice on that eye. It's already turning black and blue."

Charlie cupped his eye as the reality of the situation drenched him with worry. How could he attend a parole meeting with a black eye and face Ally's family like the respectable man they'd once known him to be? "I don't have time. I have to get to my parole meeting."

The guard snickered. "Good luck, pal."

Charlie rushed out of the cafeteria and sped down the hallway, suffocating the frustration flaming within him. Somehow, he had to prove that he was more than a criminal.

A COOL SPRING wind swirled around MacKenna Christensen's heels as she stepped out of her truck and picked up her briefcase, looping the strap over her shoulder. She waited for her roommate to get out, then rushed across the parking lot toward a two-story building with a faded redbrick exterior. Black graffiti covered the chipped wooden sign welcoming visitors to the Department of Corrections.

Lifting her lanyard, she held her ID badge in front of a machine, waiting for the *beep* before she swung the door open and stepped inside the building. She held the door open for Jen, only to realize her roommate was standing in the middle of the parking lot texting on her phone.

MacKenna tapped her heel against the faded linoleum. "Will you hurry up? I want to check my mail." She'd been gone on vacation all last week, finally taking paid time off for the first time in five years. It felt great to get away, but now that she was back, her anxiety was rising. A lot could've happened in a week. Roxanne might have relapsed. Jason could've stopped going to AA. Chase might have gone back to prison.

Jen's thumbs typed across the screen before she tossed her bright pink phone back into her overstuffed purse. Walking inside the open doorway, she put her hands on MacKenna's shoulders. "Chill. You didn't miss anything."

"You don't know that for sure."

"Yes, I do. Nothing exciting ever happens around here."

"You promise none of my clients were arrested?"

"Yes." Jen dropped her hands as they made their way toward the main office. Hushed voices carried down the long, narrow hallway. Up ahead, parole and probation officers filed into the lounge.

MacKenna rolled her eyes. "I bet Warren brought in breakfast pizzas again. What's the point of having a wellness program if no one meets their fitness goals?"

Jen shrugged. "I'll just burn off the calories during kickboxing." She stepped forward, putting a hand on her hip. "Are you coming?"

"No, I want to check my mailbox. And I'm not that hungry. I already had egg whites."

"Please, like that counts as a real breakfast." Jen pointed a manicured finger in her direction. "One of these days, you're going to wither away, and you'll wish you'd eaten more pizza."

MacKenna laughed. "When that happens, I'll let you say that you were right."

"Deal. See you later, Mac." She walked ahead, her fire red hair bouncing across her shoulders.

Smirking, Mac turned the corner. One quick peek at

her mailbox to check her files. Then she could relax a little, knowing all her clients were staying out of trouble.

She made a beeline for the office. A sudden weight smacked against her shoulder. She stumbled backward down the main hallway and met Robert's gaze. Extending his arm, he held a paper coffee cup away from his body. Brown stains were splattered across his white T-shirt and his parole officer lanyard.

She cleared her throat. "I'm so sorry. I wasn't looking."

"You owe me." Robert gave her a teasing grin as voices from the lounge amplified. He glanced down the hallway before returning his gaze to her. His grin quickly faded and his eyebrows furrowed together. "Did you hear what happened?"

"No." She drew out the word, slightly confused. Maybe Warren hadn't brought in breakfast pizzas after all. "What's going on?"

"Gabe got fired."

Her eyes widened. "Why?"

"I think it has something to do with one of his parolees."

"Hey." The deep timbre of Warren's voice carried down the hall as he stepped out of the lounge, cupping his hands on both sides of his mouth. "I'm only going to say this once, so get in here."

Sighing, Mac followed Robert as they turned away

from the office, abiding by their supervisor's orders. In the crowded lounge, she squeezed in beside Jen and Robert, standing shoulder to shoulder.

Warren waddled to an open spot next to the fridge. His dark umber skin glistened below the bright fluorescent lighting as he stopped and stuck two fingers in his mouth, whistling. He addressed the room once it was quiet. "Following a thorough investigation, Gabe lost his job yesterday." A dark sweat spot spread down the neckline of his tan button-down shirt. He gripped the shirt, airing it out. "I never thought you'd need a reminder, but romantic relationships with clients are strictly prohibited."

Jen leaned closer to Mac. "I wonder if Gabe was seeing Sheyenne Wesley. They seemed really close."

Mac wrinkled her nose. What was Gabe thinking? A parolee needed professional help to get her life back on track, not a parole officer who couldn't keep his priorities straight.

Warren whistled again, his steel-gray eyes scanning the crowded room. "If I ever catch wind of such a thing, you'll lose your job in corrections for good. Got it?"

Mac nodded. She almost laughed at the very thought. Relationships were trouble anyway. A drain on emotions and a waste of time. Why would anyone risk a career for *that*?

MAC RUSHED OUT of the crowded room, her briefcase bumping against her hip as she dashed inside the dark office. Her gaze rested on a tall stack of papers piled on Jen's desk as she flipped on the light. It looked like her roommate had a lot of work to do today.

Not that Jen would get to it anytime soon. She was still in the lounge, her enduring nosiness surely getting the best of her.

Passing Jen's desk, Mac stopped in front of the wooden cubbies on the far side of the office and grabbed the papers inside her cubby. She held the stack against her stomach, flipping through page after page, and quickly scanning the contents.

Jen was right. No arrests. No new charges. Same old, same old.

The tension in her neck loosened slightly. Her worries never went away completely, even when she'd been in Mexico, thousands of miles away from work. But that was the problem—being a parole officer wasn't just about work; it was about helping people change their lives for the better. In the last five years, she'd never been able to figure out how to get rid of the pressure, or maybe the problem was she didn't want to. Either way, she had an important role to uphold and she wanted to do her job well.

The office door creaked open and Warren shuffled inside, huffing. He pressed a clenched fist against his chest. "You're a hard person to catch."

"I was just checking to see if any changes were made to my caseload."

"That's what I need to talk to you about." He waved for her to follow him into his office.

As she stepped inside, Warren closed the door and walked behind his desk, easing into a chair. It gave a gentle swoosh under the pressure of his weight. "You have a new client."

Her head jerked up. "I do?"

"There are a couple of things I wanted to tell you, so I figured I'd give you this in person." He picked up a manila folder on his cluttered desk, handing it to her. "I hate to do this after you just got back, but with Gabe gone, we're spread thin right now."

Nodding, she took the file and opened it, reading the cover sheet. *Client name: Charles Grimm … Date of sentencing: December 16th … 32 years old … 2230 Glenn Creek Road, Maple Valley, Iowa.*

After reading her new client's bio, she glanced at the picture in the top corner of the cover sheet. Her hand flew to her mouth. Even in a jumpsuit, Charles looked just like the preppy pretty boy she remembered: gelled hair, flawless skin, and perfectly balanced features.

Lifting the strap of her briefcase over her head, she

dropped it on the floor and slumped into a chair across from Warren's desk. A lump lodged in her throat. She didn't technically know Charles Grimm, but she knew enough about him to be certain of one thing: she didn't want him on her caseload.

Warren picked up a toothpick off his desk, letting it hang out of the corner of his mouth. "Everything okay, kiddo?"

No. Absolutely not. Another parole officer would be a better fit for him. The words were supposed to come out, but her mouth was too dry to speak.

She swallowed the lump in her throat as images from Charles's car accident resurfaced. Her memories of that night were as vivid as a recurring dream: the lifeless woman's white cocktail dress soaked in blood; her bare legs covered with gashes that trailed down to her high heels; her cold, blank stare unaware of the horrific scene that ended her life.

With trembling hands, Mac shut the file and set it on Warren's desk, sliding it far away from her. She tried to keep her voice steady as she spoke. "I don't understand. I haven't had time to do any preliminary work."

"I handled all of it. While you were on vacation, I contacted Charlie's brother and checked out the living situation. Daniel and Hannah Grimm's house will be a great place for Charlie to live during his parole."

"You're on a first-name basis with him?"

"Yeah. I've known Charlie's family for a long time. They moved to Maple Valley when his dad opened Charger's Sporting Goods downtown. Charlie is the one who got me interested in golf."

"Oh."

Warren leaned forward, his stomach pressing against his desk as he took the toothpick out of his mouth and twirled it between his fingers. "Something wrong?"

She opened her mouth to explain, to tell Warren that she would never view Charlie as anything but a reckless man who had played a role in his wife's death. But she couldn't tell her supervisor that. She'd never given up on any of her clients, especially before she'd met them.

And yet, Charlie's case was different. She'd never had a client charged with a crime that resulted in death. Because of his irrevocable decisions, his wife would never live another day. Never laugh or smile. Never teach another art class or read another picture book to her students.

Mac met Warren's gaze, noticing the dark gray bags under his heavily lidded eyes. The poor guy looked like he'd barely slept, and he probably hadn't, not after firing Gabe.

She grabbed Charlie's file, running her thumb along the edge. Warren didn't deserve to deal with anything else right now. Maybe she could wait a few weeks before requesting Charlie off of her caseload. That way she could have a couple of meetings and get to know him. It would give Warren time to handle Gabe's mess, and it would give her time to find a reasonable explanation for her request.

"Is something wrong?" Warren asked again.

She slid the file into the outside pocket of her briefcase. Straightening, she looked at her supervisor, pushing her shoulders back. "Everything's good."

"You sure?"

"Yeah."

Warren stopped fiddling with his toothpick, his expression serious. "Look, Charlie's made some bad mistakes, but he's a good guy. I wouldn't want anyone else to have him except my favorite workaholic."

She tucked a strand of hair behind her ear. Warren was clearly biased toward Charlie. She'd have to find a good reason to get him removed from her caseload. It might not be enough to tell Warren she'd witnessed the car accident.

Surely after meeting her client she would find something to say. It couldn't be that hard. After all, he was the driver who'd caused the car crash, killing his wife.

Chapter 2

TRAVELERS SWARMED IN and out of the bus station, clutching cell phones in their hands. Charlie maneuvered through the crowd, his stomach knotting. His throat tightened and his mouth filled with saliva. Holding a hand to his mouth, he scrambled toward a bush. He bent over, pressing his hands on his knees as he heaved above it. Pain burned through his stomach like hot coals in a fire. People stopped to stare before rushing away.

Charlie spit into the grass. The parole board thought that living at home, in a familiar setting, would be helpful for him to acclimate from prison to everyday life. They were wrong. Being back in Maple Valley was like tearing off a scab, exposing the raw anguish scraping at his insides.

A familiar Ferrari sped down the street, whipping into the parking lot. Music boomed from the subwoofers, causing several heads to turn and watch the black sports car back up into an open spot. His brother cut off a group of teenagers walking across the lot. One of the girls held up her middle finger. Daniel returned the girl's gesture and stepped out of his vehicle dressed in a dark pinstripe suit.

Frowning, Charlie ran his hand over the stubble on his chin. Loose strands of hair fell into his face. He reached for the elastic band and retied his hair into a low ponytail as he strode across the parking lot.

Daniel glanced in his direction, then looked away. Charlie almost laughed. His brother didn't recognize him.

Once Charlie was closer to the Ferrari, Daniel looked at him again, removing a pair of Oakley sunglasses. His brother's eyes grew wide as recognition crossed his face, followed by a series of emotions: surprise, disgust, and contempt. "You look like a hippie on steroids."

Charlie's lips formed a thin, tight line. "Good to see you, too."

"Hey, I was just letting you know. They probably don't have mirrors in prison."

"They do."

Daniel made a hmph noise. "Trying to fit, then?"

"Something like that."

Daniel slid his sunglasses back over his face. "I have to get back to work. Ready to go?" Without waiting for an answer, he opened his car door and slid into the driver's seat. The car rumbled to life, piercing the air with heavy metal music.

Charlie ducked inside the car, bending his long legs to fit into the tiny space. The interior of the car caved in around him, pressing against his chest. It looked much like the sports car he used to own. The connection prodded him like a needle, injecting him with the last memory he had of driving it. If only he could go back in time to save Ally's life, so he didn't have to live another day without her.

His brother drove out of the bus station and turned onto a two-lane highway, accelerating to merge with traffic. Charlie clutched the armrest and checked the speedometer. 80 mph in a 55 mph zone.

He shuddered as Daniel leaned back in his seat, holding the steering wheel loosely with one hand. "Ready for your parole meeting tomorrow?"

Charlie squeezed the back of his neck. "Guess so."

"Warren said your parole officer is one of his best."

"You talked to Warren?"

"Yeah, he came over to inspect my house. He had to make sure it met all of the parole requirements." Daniel rolled his eyes. "That guy is such a stickler. I'm not getting rid of all the alcohol in my house just because you're living with me."

Charlie pursed his lips. "Did Warren say anything else about my parole officer?"

"Her name's MacKayla or something like that.

Sounds a little soft, if you ask me." Daniel turned the wheel, veering off of the highway.

Charlie gulped as the car slowed and they drove past a brown sign with curly green lettering. *Welcome to Maple Valley. Population 1,542.* Passing through downtown, familiar faces stopped to watch as the car teetered across the uneven redbrick street. He glanced at Val's Diner before quickly looking away. Every Saturday morning he'd eaten breakfast at the restaurant with Ally, her parents, and her brother.

His chest constricted. If only he could take away the family's sorrow and bear it all on his own. But he couldn't take away their pain any more than he could change the past.

The ache in his chest tightened, making it difficult to breathe. No doubt Ally's family wanted him to suffer. He couldn't blame them. For the rest of his life, regret would fester inside of him as a reminder of his reckless decisions and the horrifying consequences. Ally deserved so much more than regret from him, but it was too late now for anything else.

BUTTONING THE TOP of his polo, Charlie pushed back his shoulders and walked through the lobby at the Department of Corrections. Surveillance cameras hummed as they followed his movements, and then stopped when he stood in front of the secretary's desk.

A shadow appeared behind a dark screen that extended from the desk to the ceiling. The secretary opened a sliding window within the screen, sending a loud screeching noise through the lobby. He gritted his teeth at the noise as a young redhead gave him a welcoming smile. She pushed long, curly strands behind her back. "Mornin'. I'm Jen. How can I help you?"

"I have a meeting with MacKenna Christensen."

"You must be Charlie." Jen leaned forward, gold dangling earrings jingling like wind chimes. "You're in good hands. She's amazing."

"That's what I hear." The knots in his stomach loosened slightly. He had to make a good impression on his parole officer. MacKenna Christensen had the power to decide how long his parole would last. According to other inmates, the officer would release him from parole once she felt confident he was ready to move on with his life.

But he didn't want to move on with his life, not without Ally. She was his high school sweetheart, his first love, the woman he was supposed to grow old with. And now she was gone. All because of him.

If only he had been the one to die instead of her.

Jen slid a clipboard through the window. "You're a little early, so go ahead and start filling out some of this paperwork."

"Okay." He took the clipboard and headed toward an empty seat, walking past a wide window with metal bars. A heavy weight pressed against his chest. After prison and now parole, he didn't feel human anymore. He was more like a dog in a cramped, fenced-in backyard.

Swallowing hard, he sat down and picked up the pen attached to the clipboard. He started writing his name when he had the sudden, sinking sensation of being watched. Glancing up, he noticed a tall, tan woman wearing a gray skirt and a stylish suit coat studying him from the hallway. Her full lips were pursed and her piercing blue eyes were analyzing him like a specimen under a microscope. As soon as he met her gaze, she looked away, her cheeks growing crimson.

Who was she, and why was she glaring at him? Before he could wonder too long, the woman walked into the main office, her black, silky hair swaying across her slender shoulders.

It didn't matter who the woman was as long as she wasn't his parole officer. And she couldn't be. Not after the good things Daniel had heard about her and the kind things Jen had said. That woman didn't look nice.

And yet, if she wasn't his parole officer, why had she been staring at him?

MAC SLUMPED AGAINST the office door, adrenaline pumping through her veins. *Holy crap.* Charlie Grimm looked way different from the night of his car accident. He was buff now. His lanky frame had filled out, and his shoulders were broad, his chest chiseled, and his face was covered in stubble. The polo he wore clung to his torso, revealing muscular biceps and forearms that flexed when he picked up the pen and clipboard. His brown hair, which used to be short and cropped, was long and straight, pulled back, all suave, like some guy modeling for a designer clothing commercial.

Charlie was hot. Annoyingly hot. So hot that she couldn't help staring at him, and when he'd caught her, she'd run into the office instead of walking over to meet him. *How embarrassing.* The meeting hadn't even started and it was already going horribly.

Clutching her stomach, she took a deep breath, trying to steady her racing heart. What the heck was wrong with her? She needed to pull it together and get this meeting over with so she could talk to Warren and request this guy off of her caseload.

Across the office, Jen leaned back in her chair. Her eyebrows rose and disappeared beneath her bangs. "You okay?"

Mac gave her roommate a forced smile. "Sure."

"You don't seem okay."

"Then why'd you ask?"

Jen held her hands up in innocence. "Sorry. I was just trying to be nice."

"I know you were." She immediately felt guilty, not meaning to be short with her roommate. It wasn't Jen's fault Mac couldn't keep her emotions in check.

Turning toward the door, she ran a hand through her hair and tugged on her suit coat. *I can do this. I will treat Charlie Grimm like any other client. I'm a professional, after all.*

She twisted the knob and opened the door, heading to the far corner of the lobby where her new client sat, one leg draped over his knee as he balanced the clipboard above it. "Mr. Grimm?"

Charlie looked up from his paperwork, his lips parting when she extended her hand. "I'm your parole officer, MacKenna Christensen. But everybody calls me Mac."

For a second, a strange expression flashed across his face, something like dread maybe, but it disappeared too fast for her to be sure. He stood up and shook her hand. "Nice to meet you."

She glanced down at his paperwork. "Are you done?"

"Yeah."

"Great. You can bring it to my office. Follow me." Turning, she strode down the hallway and unlocked a door a few feet away. She held the door open and stepped back, allowing him to pass. As he walked by, she couldn't help noticing how nicely his dress pants fit around his narrow waist.

Redirecting her thoughts, she sat down behind her desk and crossed her legs. "Have a seat. We have a lot to get through today."

She handed him more paperwork and described what parole would be like: they would meet twice a week in different locations—at the Department of Corrections, his future workplace, and his brother's house. "In addition to our meetings, you should apply for six to eight jobs a day. You'll need documentation to prove that you've applied. And you must get a job within a month."

He leaned forward, resting his elbows on his legs. "How long does it usually take to find a job? After being charged with a crime, I mean."

"I can't say. It's different from person to person, and I've never had a client who committed the same crimes you did."

"Oh."

Mac picked up a pencil on her desk and rubbed her thumb across the lead. "Everyone in Maple Valley knows you were charged with vehicular homicide. It might be hard for employers to see past your crime, especially since they probably knew your wife." Despite her gentle delivery, even she could hear the bitterness in her voice.

Charlie shifted in his chair and cracked his knuckles. "I wish I could take it all back."

She dropped the pencil in her hand. It rolled to the edge of her desk and dropped to the floor with a light thud. "Which part? The speeding? The faulty brakes? Or the empty bottle of Jack Daniels?"

"I don't know where that bottle came from. It wasn't mine. Didn't you read the police report?"

Her defenses rose, like hair on the back of a dog's neck. The guy was obviously lying. "It said you refused to take a breathalyzer."

His nostrils flared. "That doesn't mean I was drinking."

"Why would you refuse a breathalyzer then?"

He sat up straight, crossing his arms, and she tried not to notice the way it made the muscles in his chest and forearms stand out. "Are you going to criticize me the entire meeting?"

The intensity of his brown eyes stole the air from her lungs, and she had to work at breathing normally to get the words out. "I'm sorry. We shouldn't be discussing your accident."

"Good, because I don't want to talk about it anymore."

"I understand." She chewed on the inside of her cheek. *Get a grip. Go through the preliminary paperwork and send him on his way before you say something you regret.*

Reaching into a nearby drawer, she pulled out a form and slid it across her desk. "This is a Parole Agreement. It outlines all the rules you need to follow."

Charlie leaned over her desk and read the form.

She silently went through the rules, giving him time to finish. No fights. No alcohol. Cooperate in treatment programs. Abide by a curfew. Obtain and maintain a job. After a couple of minutes had passed, she spoke again. "If you break any of these rules, you'll go back to prison."

She waited for Charlie to respond. Most clients didn't like this part—finding out they had more restrictions. She didn't blame them, especially after recently being freed from prison, but the rules were in place to prevent clients from reoffending. Nonetheless, they usually argued with her, claiming they would never make the same mistakes twice.

But Charlie said nothing. Impressed, she picked up the Parole Agreement and flipped it over to the backside. "You need to read the special conditions as well."

A moment went by before his eyes widened, and he looked up from the form. "Get my driver's license? Is that negotiable?"

"No, it's not."

"It's just that … "

"This isn't debatable." So much for being impressive.

But of all things for him to complain about, why was he upset about getting his license? She wasn't telling him he had to drive. In fact, she'd rather not have someone as reckless as him driving.

She picked up a pen from her rotating container and held it out to him. "Sign the form."

His Adam's apple bobbed up and down as a painful expression crossed his downturned face. He ran a hand through his hair, his voice hitching as he spoke. "You don't understand."

Suddenly there was a lump in her throat and she couldn't swallow it. Was he trying to make her feel sorry for him? If so, it was sort of working. But she couldn't give in, no matter how she felt. Rules were rules.

She lifted her chin and said with a steady voice, "If you can't agree to these terms, you'll go back to prison. What are you going to do?"

Chapter 3

CHARLIE KICKED THE sheets off of the bed with his bare feet. Sweat trickled down his back. He rolled over onto his stomach and rested his head against the feather-stuffed pillow, closing his eyes. Behind dark lids, his last memory of Ally replayed, refusing to let him sleep—Ally lying motionless against the car seat. The searing pain boiling beneath his ribs as he propped an elbow on her armrest and placed his ear against her mouth. Flinging the armrest out of the way, he wrapped his arms around her and held her close to his chest, waiting for a breath that never came.

He opened his eyes and turned over onto his back, wishing the memory would dissipate. It didn't. The memory clung to him as sticky as the sweat still dripping down his back.

It would never go away, and driving would only make it worse. Mac had some nerve. No way would he drive. After the accident, he'd promised himself that he would never, ever get behind the wheel of a car again.

Driving was a personal matter. But she acted like there were no boundaries. Her ridiculous list of rules gave her ultimate authority, especially now that he'd signed the Parole Agreement.

Mac was probably one of those officers who wanted the job just so she could have power over others. Trying to impress her was going to be a lot harder than he'd anticipated. But he had to try. If he didn't, she could extend his parole, or worse, send him back to prison. She'd made that quite clear.

But how could he impress someone who had judged him before they'd even met? That cold, hard glare in the lobby had said it all. She didn't like him, and she wasn't going to act like she did. He'd hoped the meeting would change her opinion, but he doubted that it did. At least she wasn't fake; he had to respect that, but so far, that was the only thing he liked about her.

Feeling wide-awake, he rolled out of bed and stumbled to the bathroom, flipping on the switch. Light flooded across the white marble sink and the obnoxiously long vanity mirror.

He peered at his reflection and ran a hand through his tousled, brown hair. He hadn't cut it since his first few weeks in prison. Not since the other inmates had ridiculed him about his *boy band hair* and labeled him as a prick. With hair reaching his shoulders, he definitely didn't look like a so-called prick anymore.

But he'd never get a job looking like a caveman.

Opening one of the vanity drawers, he pulled out a pair of scissors. He held a long strand of hair between his fingers, and after sucking in a breath, he cut it. The strand drifted into the sink, curling around the drain.

He continued cutting in quick, successive movements. With each snap of the scissors, his head and mood felt lighter, as if cutting his hair was freeing him from his ties to prison.

When he was done, he evaluated his work, watching the reflection of his hand move across his short, dark hair.

A smile tugged at his lips. He'd probably need a professional to touch it up before he went in for a job interview, but for now, it would do.

He picked up the loose strands of hair mounting in the sink. When he looked up, he fixed his gaze on the pair of unrecognizable, empty eyes.

Clutching the edge of the vanity, he lowered his chin to his chest. A new haircut wouldn't fool anyone. He was still a monster.

"KICK FASTER. PUNCH harder." The kickboxing instructor paced across the gym floor, his stocky image reflecting on the four mirrored walls.

Mac swooped behind the swinging punching bag, leaning away at just the right angle before she kicked at it with a powerful roundhouse. The bag swung back and forth.

Tucker Williams punched the bag in front of him, his arm muscles bulging beneath his navy Maple Valley Police T-shirt. He shuffled from side to side, glancing over at Mac, then Jen. "So I have to ask … Did one of your POs really sleep with an offender?"

Nodding, Jen crouched down and retied her shoes. "Apparently, Gabe threatened his client, telling her if she told anyone, he'd send her back to prison."

Mac's eyes widened. "Are you sure that's true?"

"That's what Robert told me in the break room yesterday. There are text messages to prove it."

Tucker shook his head. "That's pathetic."

"And you wished something exciting would happen in Maple Valley," said Mac.

Jen stood and slipped her hands back into a pair of pink kickboxing gloves. She smirked. "I should be careful what I wish for, huh?"

"No kidding. Next time you make a wish, make sure it doesn't affect the rest of us." Mac jabbed at her bag, releasing some of the adrenaline pumping through her body. She didn't actually blame Jen, but her meeting with Charlie had left her on edge. "I wouldn't have Charlie Grimm on my caseload if Gabe hadn't been fired."

Tucker scratched his head. "That name sounds familiar."

"Was the meeting with Charlie that bad?" Jen asked.

Mac swung a right hook in the air, missing her moving target. "It was horrible," she admitted. What an understatement. It was the worst parole meeting she'd led and the most unprofessional she'd ever acted with a client. But dang it, she couldn't help it.

Her new client was the kind of guy who made her blood boil—attractive, self-assured, and stubborn. Not a good combination. Part of her *did* appreciate the way he'd dressed up for the meeting, wearing a polo and pleated slacks, and yet, did he really think his money would impress her?

She tightened the straps on her gloves, just above the Velcro. "Charlie's a jerk. He claims that the empty bottle of alcohol in *his* car wasn't his."

"Oh, I remember him." Tucker steadied the punching bag. "He's the guy I arrested that night when you were with me, Mac."

Jen stopped moving. "You witnessed his car accident?"

"Yeah, we were on our way to arrest one of Mac's clients." Tucker picked up a small rag lying on the floor and wiped at the sweat trickling down his bald head. His expression turned sober as he glanced at Mac. "That was an intense night. We saw everything: the car speeding through the traffic light, the collision, and that woman's dead body."

Shuddering, Mac grabbed a water bottle from her gym bag, tilting her head back for a drink. She should have swallowed her pride and told Warren the truth. She couldn't look past Charlie's mistakes.

How could she? Charlie had been drinking and driving, and his wife had paid the consequences. While he could move on with his life, Ally Grimm lay buried in the ground, serving a life sentence.

The water bottle crackled beneath her tightening grip. "I'll never be able to look at Charlie without thinking about what he did."

Jen flung her pale arm at the bag, her fist causing little movement. "You better be careful. You wouldn't want Charlie to file a complaint against you. It could hurt your chances to win the Outstanding Correctional Worker award."

Mac almost dropped her water bottle. Earning the highest esteemed award would be a dream come true, but winning it so early in her career didn't seem possible. "I highly doubt I'll get nominated this year."

"Are you kidding me? You created a new reentry program for ex-offenders, you co-wrote the Substance Abuse Recognition program, and you just won the Proud Parenting grant. Think of how many delinquent parents you've impacted by allowing them to learn better parenting skills."

Her cheeks flushed. "There are several good candidates who have also worked hard to make changes in corrections this year."

"True, but Warren doesn't call anyone else his favorite workaholic. I'm sure he'd recommend you over anyone else."

Mac bit back a smile, allowing the possibility to take root. She didn't do any of those things to win an award; she did them because she wanted to make a difference in peoples' lives. But winning the Outstanding Correctional Worker award would be a lifetime achievement.

She sent a succession of punches at the bag. If Jen was right and she had any chance of winning, she'd have to hold her tongue around Charlie until she requested him off of her caseload.

MAC REACHED FOR her briefcase and stepped out of the state car, staring up at Daniel Grimm's house. The architecture of the mansion closely resembled an old Victorian home. The black roof peaked and slanted at different angles above the white siding. Large, rectangular windows overlooked a manicured yard with tall bushes built as a barrier between their house and the neighbors on both sides.

Walking up to the house, she pressed a hand to her twisting stomach. Today's meeting should be easy. It was a simple house check to get a better understanding of Charlie's home life. She'd check out the house and ask a few questions about job applications, and it would be over. Then she could talk to Warren and request Charlie off of her caseload. Easy peasy, if her nerves would just settle down.

Charlie opened the door, clean-shaven, dressed in jeans and a black button-down shirt with the top few buttons undone and the sleeves casually pushed up. His hair was shorter, highlighting his dark features. Somehow, he looked even hotter than before. "Good morning."

"Same to you," she said breathlessly.

He stepped back into the entryway. "Come on in."

Heat rose to her cheeks as she directed her gaze away from him and stepped into a spacious entryway with shiny wood flooring. A sparkling, crystal-studded chandelier hung from a high, vaulted ceiling, and a few feet away from the front doors, a spiral staircase led to the second floor.

She tightened her jaw to keep her mouth from falling open. Who needed this much space in one house? They probably had rooms they never used.

Charlie eyed her carefully as if trying to read her

thoughts. "My brother likes to keep up with the Joneses. I think it's a little over-the-top."

She tilted her head. Why would anyone who grew up in the same neighborhood think like that? Maybe he wasn't as pretentious as she'd thought.

Charlie turned and walked down a spacious hallway. "This way."

As she followed him, she caught a whiff of his body soap, musky and fresh. It shouldn't have smelled good to her, but it did, and it sent a light, airy sensation fluttering through her chest. Her gaze traveled up and down his body, the way his jeans fit snugly over his hips, his lean torso, and broad shoulders. Could Charlie get any better looking?

Then she remembered. He was reckless. And because of his reckless decisions, he'd gone to prison and ended up on her parole. He was the last guy she should find attractive.

At the back of the house, he walked into a sunroom with wicker end tables and sofas. On one of the tables sat two steaming cups of coffee and a platter with milk, cream, and sugar.

He reached for a cup. "Want some?"

"Yeah."

"How do you take it?"

"Black."

He handed her the warm cup. Steam spiraled between them as they sat down on the sofas across from one another. There was something intriguing about the way his shirt highlighted his muscles, and the masculine soap scent filling the room, making her want to lean in closer and take a deep whiff of it.

Determined to squash her attraction, she placed her briefcase on the floor and brought the cup to her lips with a shaky hand. The warm liquid caressed her throat. She took another sip and set the cup on a wicker end table. Opening her briefcase, she slid to the edge of the sofa and looked at Charlie. "Do you have the notes I requested, to prove you're looking for jobs?"

"Yeah." He reached for a stack of papers lying on the floor. Bending over to grab them, his jeans grew tight around his thighs. She directed her gaze away from his waist as he handed her the papers. "I filled out applications for banks and accounting firms."

She skimmed through the applications, frowning. "Would you consider applying at a grocery store or a fast food restaurant? They might be easier to get than some of the jobs you've applied for."

His lips drew into a thin line. Leaning forward, he reached for the other cup of coffee and mixed in cream and sugar with a spoon. He took a drink and looked at her, his eyes flashing with determination. "I used to be the financial analyst at Charger's Sporting Goods."

"Sometimes you have to start at the bottom of the

totem pole, then work your way up."

Charlie lifted his head and she noticed a small dimple in the middle of his chin. "I like to be challenged."

She lowered the papers and glared at him. He also liked *being* a challenge. "Right now, any job is better than no job."

Charlie set down his coffee cup with a light thud. "I get that, but I'm still going to apply for finance and accounting positions too."

"Fine. Call me if you hear back from an employer."

"What's wrong with having high expectations? At my first meeting you said you didn't know how my application process would go."

She opened her mouth to tell Charlie that he should feel lucky his biggest problem was trying to find a decent job. It could be worse—he could have lost his life, like his wife had. After a minute, she finally spoke, keeping her tone even. "Apply where you want, but remember, you need to have a job within a month."

"Okay. But I still have one concern."

"What?"

He stared down at his hands and cracked his knuckles before meeting her gaze. "I want to wait to get my driver's license."

She shook her head. "I told you that wasn't negotiable."

"I know. I'd just like to wait a few weeks."

She restacked the papers on her lap. "I tell all of my clients to get a driver's license because it looks better to employers if you have one."

"Oh. You don't care if I drive?"

She bit her lip. "I want you to get your license, but it's up to you if you decide to drive again."

Nodding, Charlie leaned forward, running a hand over his clean-shaven face. Sunlight poured in from the window, accentuating his expression—a mixture of sadness and regret that brought with it a sudden ache she hadn't expected. "What's wrong?"

"Nothing. I couldn't be better. I'm a grown man who's scared of driving."

"You don't have to be so sarcastic," she said in a quiet tone.

Charlie dropped his hands and lifted his head, meeting her gaze. "I know you won't understand, but I don't want to drive ever again. I can't take the risk of hurting someone."

Her eyes widened. "That's why? You don't want to hurt anyone else?"

"Yeah. Why do you sound so surprised?"

"I just thought … " Mac crossed her legs and looked down at her lap, straightening the creases on her dress pants. She'd thought Charlie's reason would be more about him. "I figured you were worried about feeling guilty."

He slumped back against the sofa. "I don't need to drive to feel guilty. I feel guilty all of the time."

A lump formed in her throat. How many times had she wished for clients to open up to her, to share their true feelings so she could understand them better?

She reached for her coffee, twisting the cup in her hands as she silently replayed Charlie's words. *I feel guilty all of the time.* He obviously felt an immense amount of regret, but there was so much more to it than that. He was hurting. And there was a part of her that wanted to make him feel better.

But she couldn't help Charlie if he was on someone else's caseload. Maybe she should reconsider going through with the request. She was supposed to meet with Warren on Monday, so she'd have to make a decision this weekend. At least she had a couple more days to think about it because with Charlie sitting nearby, his masculine body soap intoxicating the room, it was hard to think straight.

SQUATTING, CHARLIE LIFTED the heavy barbell on his shoulders. He clenched his teeth together and stood, heaving the bar high above his head. The muscles in his shoulders strained and shook, and sweat trickled down his warm face. He slowly lowered the bar and let it hang in front of his waist for a second before squatting again and doing a set of bicep curls.

The doorbell rang, its chimes echoing through the basement. He dropped the bar to the floor, rushing up the stairs. Loud, insistent knocks banged on the front door. He hustled into the foyer, flinging the front door open. A familiar, gangly teenager stood on the front porch wearing sweatpants and a gold Iowa Hawkeyes sweatshirt. TJ lifted his chin, dark eyes staring sullenly at Charlie.

He took a step back into the foyer, squeezing the back of his neck. "TJ, what are you doing here?"

A Jack Russell darted inside the house. The small dog U-turned around the coatrack, his nails clicking against the polished wood floor. Wagging his brown and white tail, he sped toward Charlie.

Jackson? A dull ache spread across his chest. He crouched down and the dog leaped onto his bent legs, licking his face.

TJ cleared his throat.

Charlie swept a hand over Jackson's back and stood, causing the dog to jump down. He stood eye to eye with TJ. The teenager must have grown a foot taller since the last time they'd seen each other. Ally would've loved to see how mature her brother looked now.

Taking a step forward, he leaned against the doorframe. "I'm so sorry, TJ, for everything."

"I didn't come to hear you apologize," TJ said in a cold, unforgiving tone.

His lips parted. Then why was TJ here, if not to get an apology, the only thing he could give?

Ally's brother narrowed his eyes. "My family is a mess because of you. My parents are depressed. My mom still has days when she won't leave the house and my dad barely talks to anyone."

Charlie sucked in a gulp of fresh air. TJ and his parents had every right to be angry, but he hated knowing how much Ally's family was still grieving. All because of his bad decisions.

The teenager glanced down at the dog. "Having Jackson just makes my parents worse. They hate him."

"He's a good dog. None of this is his fault."

TJ shrugged. "I've taken care of him because he was Ally's pet, but I can't do it anymore."

"What are you going to do with him then?"

Lifting his chin, TJ crossed his arms. "Will you take him?"

His eyes widened. "What?"

"I want you to keep him." TJ pulled a leash out of the front pocket of his sweatshirt.

Pushing off the doorframe, Charlie shifted his weight from one foot to the other. "I don't know … "

"I've thought about giving him to the pound."

"Don't do that."

"Does that mean you'll take him?"

Jackson whined and his perky brown ears drooped. He lay down on top of Charlie's shoe, tucking his paws beneath his brown and white head.

He pinched the bridge of his nose. Keeping Jackson would bring up too many memories of Ally. It would deepen the open wound around his heart, scarring it beyond repair.

And yet, if he didn't keep the dog, TJ would take Jackson to the pound and his energetic dog would be stuck behind bars, waiting for a family to adopt him. Or worse, Jackson would be put to sleep if no one chose him.

TJ extended his arm, holding out the leash. "Well, are you taking Jackson or not?"

He stared down at the leash. This was about so much more than keeping his dog. He didn't want to make one more decision that he'd regret.

•

Chapter 4

MAC SET HER laptop on Roxanne's cluttered kitchen table, sandwiching it between a half-eaten bowl of cereal and a cracked plate with toast on top. Opening her computer, she peered over the screen at her client. "What are your long-term goals?"

Roxanne loosened the hair tie at the back of her head and slipped the elastic band around her small wrist. Greasy, blond strands fell across her slender face. "I just have one."

"Which is?"

"I want custody of my kids."

She gave her client a sad smile. "That's a great goal."

Slumping against her chair, Roxanne pressed trembling fingers into her temples. "Do you think it's possible?"

She pursed her lips. Roxanne didn't have to say she was afraid of failing her children. Again. Most clients were afraid of messing up their second chances—in their marriages, in their families, in society. Fear was always present in their eyes.

If only she could deny the fear she'd seen in Charlie's eyes when he'd told her that he was afraid of driving. Her heart still ached when she remembered his hard, downcast eyes, deep shaky voice, and white knuckled hand running through his hair.

Disgust piled up like a dam in her chest. She wasn't supposed to feel sorry for Charlie.

Not when his bad decisions made it evident that he was a careless husband who knew better.

Roxanne leaned forward, setting her bony elbows on the table. "Well, is it? Is it possible to get my kids back?"

"Yes, but you have to earn a steady income first. Your kids need stability." At least she didn't have to convince Charlie to find a good job. She almost smiled. So she could find a positive attribute about him, after all.

Blinking, Roxanne looked over Mac's shoulder. She followed her client's gaze, glancing at school pictures hanging on the fridge of three young girls with toothless grins.

"You know, my kids were just fine before you people came along and sent me to prison." Her client's chair skidded across the faded linoleum as she stood up and marched across the small kitchen. "I should have custody of them no matter what. They're my kids."

"But they need a stable parent."

"They had one. I made money."

Mac ran her tongue over her front teeth. How many times had she heard that rationalization from her own parents? "You made money selling illegal drugs."

"That money paid for clothes, food, and shelter. Wasn't that enough?"

She rubbed her thumb against the worn table, picking off a dried noodle. No, it wasn't enough. Roxanne might have provided the basics, but her kids needed more. Her own parents had said they'd provided her with enough. But a light jacket in the cold of winter had not kept her warm. Ten dollars to buy fast food had not satisfied her growling stomach. A TV had not filled the void while her parents were out getting drunk.

Roxanne pounded her small fist against the yellowed countertop. "How much longer are you gonna come into my apartment and judge me?"

"I'm not judging you. I'm helping you get your life together, so you can get your kids back."

"See this?" Her client picked up a handcrafted mug off the countertop. She tapped on the cup where *The World's Best Mom* was scrawled across the middle. "My kids think I'm a good mom. So you can shove your judgmental thoughts right up your—"

"Why don't you sit down and we can talk like civilized adults?"

Roxanne lifted the mug to her lips with a shaky hand. She took a sip, keeping her angry, narrowed eyes on Mac.

"Please?"

Her shaky hand loosened around the mug. It slipped out of her fingers.

Shooting out of her chair, Mac leaned forward, arm outstretched as she reached for the cup. Her fingertips grazed the porcelain. The mug hit the floor, sending broken pieces skidding across the linoleum. Black tea spread in a small wave between their feet.

"Look what you made me do. Sarah made that for me in art class."

"Maybe we can glue it back together." She stood next to her client, resisting the urge to comfort her. After firing Gabe, Warren was on high alert. Even clients thinking they could become friends went beyond the boundary of a client/officer relationship. She couldn't afford to take chances. "I have an idea. Why don't you shower, I'll clean up the floor, and then I'll drop you off downtown to apply for jobs?"

Roxanne stared at the mess on the floor. "I probably shouldn't tell you this, but I sold dope to lots of people around here. They keep asking me when I'm gonna get back in business."

"And what do you tell them?"

"To leave me alone, but it don't matter. They'll just keep asking."

"You're right. You have to ignore them, like you've

been doing."

"Whatever. But I better get my kids back when parole is over."

"I hope you will," she said in a quiet voice.

Roxanne stepped over the broken pieces of porcelain on the floor and turned to face her with her chin held high. "I really was a good mom. It's the only thing I was ever good at."

As her client's feeble body disappeared down the hallway, Mac squeezed her eyes shut. Even though Roxanne had made mistakes in the past, at least she wanted custody of her kids. Not all children were so lucky. Her parents had never wanted her. As a child, her dad would get drunk and then tell her that she was a mistake. His slurred words shouldn't have mattered, but they did—then and now. It still pricked her heart to know her parents didn't want anything to do with her.

CHARLIE WHIPPED HIS arm forward, throwing the ball across the dog park. Jackson darted into the grass, a pug and beagle chasing after him.

"Bruno, come here." The familiar voice came from a woman standing nearby.

Charlie turned to find Mac kneeling on the pavement with a small bag of dog treats in her hand. A beagle waddled over to her as she handed him a treat and kissed the top of the dog's head. His eyebrows rose. The no-nonsense parole officer had a soft side?

Mac tilted her head and caught him looking at her. "Oh, hi Charlie."

His gaze traveled over her body: dark Keds, tattered blue jeans, loose T-shirt half sliding off one shoulder, ebony hair tied up in a messy ponytail. *Dang.* She looked so cute and sexy at the same time, he had a hard time looking away as he strolled toward her.

"What?" She tugged at her shirt, holding out the bottom and glancing down at the Led Zeppelin logo. "Do I have a stain or something?"

Trying to recover, he slid his hands in his pockets and leaned back on his heels. "No, I'm just surprised you're a fan of rock music."

"Why?"

"I don't know many women who listen to it." He gave her a playful smile. "But you are a parole officer. Maybe I shouldn't be surprised you like stuff a little tougher than the norm." As the words tumbled out, he wondered if he'd offended her.

She eyed him carefully before a light smile played across her lips. "I'm pretty sure most clients think that, but you're the first person to say it to my face. In fact, I think most clients expect me to be some meaty, butch woman."

"That might have crossed my mind." Returning her smile, Charlie glanced away, scanning the grassy area for Jackson. He put two fingers in his mouth and whistled to get the dog's attention.

Jackson's ears perked up as he ran back and jumped up on Charlie's leg, ball caught firmly in his mouth. Charlie grabbed the ball, threw it again, and Jackson dashed away.

"Is that your brother's dog?" she asked.

"No, he's mine."

"Oh. Did you just get him?"

He ran a hand over the stubble on his jaw. "Ally's brother gave him back to me a couple of days ago."

"You don't seem too thrilled."

"If I didn't take Jackson, her brother would've taken him to the pound. So I didn't have much of a choice."

"You always have a choice," she said quietly.

Charlie stiffened. Did she mean his choices? He locked on to Mac's unwavering gaze, her eyes demanding a response. "Like when I made all the wrong ones and lost my wife?"

"I didn't say that."

"No, but that's what you meant."

She opened her mouth, then shut it, obviously at a loss for words.

What was her problem? Before he could say something he regretted, he walked to a nearby bench and sat down, heat rising up the back of his neck. This wasn't a parole meeting he had to sit through, and he wasn't going to take her condescending attitude.

Leaning forward, he set his elbows on his knees as Bruno waddled over to where she was standing. As she leaned over and fed another treat to him, her shirt lifted, exposing an intricate, colorful tattoo of a fish. Judging from the looks of the tattoo, it probably extended up most of her back. He wondered what it symbolized.

As if sensing his thoughts, she pulled her shirt lower over her jeans and walked to the bench. As she sat next to him, he caught the scent of wildflowers. She leaned back in the glow of the late-afternoon sun, the bright rays giving her dark hair a reddish tone and highlighting her tan skin so it had a bronze glow.

He leaned back against the bench and her blue eyes softened, gentler than before. "I'm sorry."

"Do you have something against me?"

She shifted, dark red blotches appearing on her neck. "It's hard for me to get over how your wife died. If you hadn't been drinking—"

"I already told you. I wasn't drinking." Charlie clenched his jaw. No one would ever believe him, but he was being honest. He had no idea where that empty bottle had come from.

"Okay." The word came out soft and uncertain.

He let out a growl. "You're unbelievable. Have you

ever tried to put yourself in your clients' shoes?"

"Yes, I have. I'm sure it's hard being released from prison, feeling like you're finally free, only to have a parole officer monitoring your every move." She lifted her chin before continuing. "It's a big change from prison to everyday life. That's one of the reasons parole was created. To help you transition."

His lips parted. Mac understood her clients better than he thought. "Now that I'm out, I can't stop thinking about what my life used to be like: the long hours at work, golfing with my friends on weekends, going to parties with Ally. I don't want to do that anymore." He stared down at his hands. "And every time I see a car, I think about that night, replaying it over and over again. It's like a bad movie."

Her eyes filled with sympathy as Jackson dashed toward the bench and jumped between them, raising his front paws on Charlie's arm and licking his face. Charlie almost smiled, but the heaviness in his chest pulled his lips into a grimace.

Mac scratched behind Jackson's ear. "I think it's good that you decided to keep your dog."

"You do?"

"Yeah. It sounds like it was a tough decision, but as Albus Dumbledore once said, 'We all must face the choice between what is right and what is easy.'"

"You like rock music *and* Harry Potter books?"

She laughed, lighthearted and unrestrained. "I've never read the books, but I've seen all the movies."

His eyes widened. Mac was very different from what he'd thought.

Moving Jackson onto his lap, he rested his arm above the back of the bench. "Which movie is your favorite?"

"I like the third one. It's the movie where Harry discovers Sirius is his godfather."

He nodded. "I give Sirius credit for being imprisoned in Azkaban. That place would be terrible."

"Oh come on. You couldn't handle dementors trying to suck the life out of you?"

He chuckled, the foreign sound reverberating in his ears. Mac seemed to take his laughter as encouragement, launching into a monologue about the Ministry of Magic's corrupt government and the incompetent officials. Maybe she wasn't such a stiff after all. In fact, as he listened to her talk, he realized that buried under all that hostility, there was a softness to her that he hadn't noticed before.

CHECKING HER INBOX, Mac responded to several emails and deleted all of her junk mail. Monday mornings were the worst. It took almost twenty extra minutes to go through emails like *10 Great Date Ideas* or *Join Our*

Dating Website for Free! How did spammers get her freaking email anyway? She didn't need one more reminder that she was single.

Minimizing her inbox, she clicked on her calendar, letting the mouse hover above today's date. Her meeting with Warren started in an hour, unless she decided to cancel it.

After talking with Charlie at the dog park, she was more confused than ever. Was he trying to make a good impression by taking interest in her, or did he actually want to get to know her?

And why did she care? It shouldn't matter. He was just a client, and yet, she had to admit that she was very intrigued by him. His openness was refreshing. The comment about female parole officers still had her smiling. But his openness also meant that he had no qualms about calling her out when she'd pressed him too far. He didn't do it in an angry way, though, like most clients would, and she had to respect that.

She moved the clicker on her computer screen, coming to a decision. Charlie was very different from her other clients. He had a good upbringing, he was motivated, confident, and he felt guilty for what he'd done. This was her opportunity to grow as a parole officer, to help someone who was definitely hurting.

It was sound, logical reasoning. She tried to convince herself that it was her only reasoning, and his good looks had nothing to do with it, but she wasn't so sure.

Setting her pointer finger on the mouse, she pressed down, deleting her meeting with Warren. Done. No going back now. She would do her job to the best of her ability.

Her phone vibrated inside the drawer of her metal desk. She pulled out the drawer and reached for her phone, seeing that she had a new voicemail. She listened to the message, her eyes widening. The voicemail was from her mom.

MacKenna, I need you. Please visit me as soon as possible. The words were music to her ears, replacing the frenetic tune of her worries with a hopeful, upbeat march.

Grabbing her purse, Mac shot out of her chair, ran into the office to tell Jen she'd be gone for the next couple of hours, and headed to the Hensworth Chemical Dependency Center.

She rushed inside the center and stopped in front of the receptionist's desk. A man wearing a counselor badge was on the phone. Eyeing Mac, he concluded the conversation and set the phone into the dock.

Leaning over the counter, she clasped her hands together. "I'm here to see Lynn Christensen."

"Are you her daughter?"

"Yes."

The man straightened, walked around the desk, and

stood in front of her. "I'm James. I'm Lynn's counselor at HCDC. I know she asked you to visit her, but … " He scratched his head. "We never advise our patients to call or see loved ones so soon."

"But she asked for me."

James furrowed his eyebrows. Wrinkles creased the skin around his tired eyes. "You don't have to do this. These meetings can be very difficult."

Most days she'd agree with him. Seeing her mom *was* difficult. But today would be different. Lynn wouldn't be drunk. Sentences wouldn't slur together and vodka wouldn't ooze from her breath. No way would she leave without talking to her mom, not if Lynn was finally sober. "I want to see her."

James scratched his head again and looked down the hall. "Lynn's in a room waiting for you. But you should know, she just went through detox. She's had a rough few days here."

"I can handle it."

"Okay, right this way." He led her down the hallway and opened the door to a small white room with a table and two chairs. "I'll leave you two alone," he said, then shut the door.

Lynn sat erect in one of the chairs, her hands twisting above the table. She'd cut her hair. Black, choppy strands stuck out at odd angles from her scalp. At least she looked clean. And she'd somehow lost weight. A red sweater hung from her thin frame.

Mac's chest tightened as a pair of blue eyes, so much like her own, looked up from the table. "Hi Lynn."

A smile flickered over her mom's pale, worn face. "You came."

She pulled out the chair across from Lynn, sitting on the edge. "It's been a while. You weren't home last time I stopped by."

"I told you not to come to the apartment. Your dad doesn't like it. He thinks you're checking up on us."

She reached across the table and squeezed Lynn's icy hands. "I'm so proud of you for being here, for asking for help."

Lynn pulled away, slumping against the back of her chair. "I don't want to be here. I don't need help."

"I'm confused. I thought you admitted yourself."

With shaky hands, Lynn lifted the bottom of her sweatpants and rolled down her tall white socks. A thin, red gash extended from her knee to her ankle.

Mac leaned forward, her eyes narrowing as she examined the cut. She pictured her dad, towering above her mom, drunkenly slicing the knife through her mom's skin as she screamed in agony. She pounded her fist against the table. "Jack did that to you, didn't he?"

Her mom shrugged. "Your dad just needs some time to cool off. You know how he is."

"That's why you came here, to get away from him?"

"I thought it'd be the safest place, but it's horrible." She pulled up her sock and rolled down her sweatpants. "I need a drink."

Her lips trembled as the ugly truth tumbled out of her mom's mouth like garbage poured from a dumpster. "If you'd just be honest with the authorities, they could help you get away from him."

"I won't do that, and I don't want you walking out of here and telling the counselors anything."

Sighing, Mac glanced down at the table. Reporting Jack's abuse wouldn't change anything unless her mom pressed charges. "Let me find you a nice apartment and Jack won't know where to find you. He'll never be able to hurt you again."

"No. He's my husband." Lynn set her feet on the chair and bent her legs in front of her chest. "I made a vow to him."

She snorted. Lynn had made a vow that bound her to a man who had ruined her life. All because she felt obligated to stick by her husband's side, to be the loyal, forgiving wife. "If you leave Jack he can go to a treatment center, too."

"You know he won't go. The only way he'd stop drinking is if he went to jail." Lynn ran a hand through her jagged hair. "And I'm not calling the police on him. Family shouldn't do that to one another." Her mom thrust the words at her like a sharp sword.

Her lungs constricted, her breath hitching. "I'm not getting into this with you. I'm just trying to help. Why can't you see that?"

Her mom gave a stilted, high-pitched laugh. "You always thought you were better than us."

Mac stood and clutched the back of her chair. Why had she thought today would be different? Being sober couldn't suddenly transform Lynn into a warmhearted mom who cared about her daughter. "Why did you ask me to come here?"

Lynn's chest rose and fell as she glanced at the door, then back at Mac. "Don't tell the counselors I asked but … will you loan me some money?"

She shook her head. She should have known better. People didn't change overnight. Lynn wasn't in treatment because she wanted to stay sober. And she certainly wasn't sorry about the past.

She walked around the table to stand in front of her mom. "I'm not giving you money. You'll just use it on alcohol when you get out of here."

"Please." Her mom reached for her hair, stroking a loose strand with her fingers. "I'll let you inside the apartment the next time you stop by."

"I'll see you later." She reached for Lynn's hand, gently pulling it away from her hair. Turning, she trudged out of the room, blinking back the moisture in her eyes. Her mom needed to realize that her life was in danger. It would only take once for Jack's anger to get so out of control that he killed her.

But Lynn was in too deep. She'd fallen for Jack in high school, and according to her, she'd been attracted to his charming personality and bad boy image. Before she figured out that Jack was just a jerk who drove a motorcycle, she'd gotten pregnant, and married him right after they graduated. Now, they were both alcoholics who could barely pay their rent.

Seeing Lynn's attachment to Jack was exactly why Mac stayed away from charming guys. It was just an act. A way to cover up who they really were.

After seeing how her mom's life had turned out, she would never fall prey to a man like that.

DANIEL GRIMM WRAPPED his arms around his wife's ample waist and pressed his lips against her warm cheek. The faint smells of vanilla perfume and chocolate chip cookies rose from her striped maternity dress. "I haven't seen Charlie around. Are we alone?" he asked.

Hannah nodded, her blond bob bouncing up and down. She reached for an open bag of shredded cheese and sprinkled it over two pieces of warm breaded chicken. "He took Jackson for a walk."

Tilting his head, Daniel trailed kisses down his wife's

cheek to her neck. “Let’s take advantage of our alone time, then.”

She wiggled out of his embrace and reached for the two plates of chicken. “Can we wait until after dinner? I’m starving.”

Daniel lowered his hands to her thighs, snugly fit in leggings. “Come on, baby.”

Turning around, Hannah rolled her eyes at him. “I wish you could understand what it’s like to be pregnant. I’ve been craving chicken all day, and I’m really hungry.”

He dropped his arms and adjusted the waist of his suit pants. If only Hannah could understand what she did to him, and how hard it was to control himself when she wasn’t in the mood. Since she’d become pregnant, her stomach had taken on a mind of its own.

With the two plates in hand, Hannah planted a kiss on his lips. “I promise I’ll make it up to you after dinner, okay?”

Nodding, he walked to the wine fridge and selected a bottle of Cabernet Sauvignon. He poured a large glass for himself and grabbed a glass of lemonade for Hannah. Following her into the dining room, he took a seat at the end of the long table.

She set down two steaming plates of chicken Parmesan and mashed potatoes, and plopped into a chair. Wasting no time, she picked up her fork and shoved a large piece of chicken in her mouth. “How was your day?"

"We interviewed four people for the up front manager position and none of them are qualified." Grabbing the glass of wine, Daniel took a long sip, savoring the dry, delicious drink.

Hannah glanced at the wine, pursing her lips. She didn't approve of keeping alcohol in the house after Warren had asked them not to. Taking another bite, she looked up at Daniel.

"What about Charlie? I thought his parole officer called you about giving him an interview."

"She did."

"So, why haven't you asked him?"

Daniel took another sip of wine, setting the almost empty glass down on the table as he considered Hannah's idea. "I'm worried about how customers would feel having an offender up front."

"But he's your brother, and everyone knows what happened was an accident."

"I'll think about it, okay?"

Annoyance flickered across her face, her kind resolve crumbling, like it usually did when she wanted to fix a lull in the conversation. "You haven't been very nice to Charlie. Can't you try a little harder to get along with him?"

"It's not that simple."

Sighing, Hannah propped her elbows on the table.

"He's been awfully distraught. He spends most of his days downstairs in our gym, pumping weights. And this morning, he went for a run, then came back and mowed our lawn, even though I told him we pay a lawn care company to do it."

Daniel took a drink of Cabernet Sauvignon, tilted his head back, and finished off the wine. Small red droplets slid back down into the glass. "I don't think he knows what to do now that he's out of prison."

"That's why he needs all the support he can get right now."

"You're making it sound like I'm the bad guy. I'm not the one who ended up in prison."

"I know, but—"

"But nothing. Everything else in his life has come easy. School, sports, work. It's about time he learns how to deal with his problems the hard way." Daniel grabbed his napkin and wiped his mouth, then tossed it on the table. "It'll be good for him."

Leaning back against her chair, Hannah set the fork down, her big, brown eyes assessing him across the table. "Sounds to me like you're jealous."

Daniel smothered a laugh, coughing into his hand. "I'm annoyed that my parents used to treat Charlie like he walked on water. Back then, according to them, he could do no wrong."

"But you have a good relationship with them, too."

"Now I do. My parents couldn't have made it without me after Charlie went to prison."

"I'm sure they were devastated."

Daniel nodded. "That's an understatement." He'd never told Hannah much about the months following Charlie's accident, but with his brother living with them, the details were bound to come out sooner or later. "My mom locked herself in her room and cried for weeks, and my dad took a leave of absence from Charger's." He paused, finally feeling the pleasant, calming effects from the wine. "My parents relied on me for everything. I went over to their house for weeks and cooked meals for them."

"They were lucky to have you." She lifted her legs, extending them on his lap.

Daniel picked up one of Hannah's feet, massaging his thumb over her bare skin. "The worst part was handling the news media. They shoved their microphones in my face every time I left my apartment."

"That's awful. I wish I could have been there for you."

Letting go of her foot, Daniel walked around the table and kneeled down beside Hannah, cupping her chin with his hand. He leaned closer and kissed her lips before tipping his head back to stare into her eyes. "You came along at just the right time. The last few years have been the best of my life."

Hannah smiled, and he let her believe she was the only reason his life had been going so well lately. But it was also because Mr. Perfect hadn't been around, overshadowing him. Without Charlie, he had gotten everything he'd ever wanted.

Hannah loosened his tie and unfastened the top two buttons of his dress shirt. "Remember that promise I made you?"

A slow smile spread across his face. "What do you have in mind?"

She yanked the tie off of his neck and unfastened the rest of the buttons on his shirt, leaving his chest exposed. "Let's go upstairs."

"I have a better idea." He bent down and hoisted her up onto the table.

She giggled and wrapped her legs around his waist. "Are you sure we should do this in here?"

Daniel ran his hands through her hair, pulling her lips to his.

The front door slammed shut.

"I'm back," Charlie called from the entryway.

As Hannah lowered her legs, Daniel groaned. "You've got to be kidding me." Charlie always managed to ruin everything. If his brother thought he'd get out of prison and everything would go back to normal, he was very wrong. No way would Daniel let his younger brother outshine him once again.

Chapter 5

CHARLIE TAPPED HIS finger on the armrest of his chair, waiting for Mac to pull up his file on the computer. As he waited, his mind drifted to the conversation he'd had with her at the dog park. They'd spent an hour on the bench, bouncing from one subject to the next—their favorite books and movies; the best places to eat downtown; his family and their business; and how he'd spent almost every weekend at Charger's, stocking shelves or running one of the cash registers. He'd told her a lot about his background, but she hadn't offered much information about herself.

Looking around her office, maybe he shouldn't be surprised. Distracted by the Parole Agreement during the first meeting, he hadn't noticed how plain her office was. The room was small with a tall bookcase, a metal file cabinet, and an old, worn desk. The walls were barren except for a bulletin board, cluttered with papers about AA meetings, signs of sexual assault, and local counseling programs. No pictures of her family or friends hung on the pale, white walls. He wondered if she was someone who didn't grow close to others easily.

Mac was very different from Ally, who loved being around people. Ally had enjoyed throwing parties for any reason, just to have an excuse to get together and celebrate. One year, she'd even thrown a party for Jackson.

His heart ached as he remembered Ally's excitement as she played hostess, and yet, he'd never really enjoyed the parties all that much. He'd gone along with her ideas just to make her happy. But if he had it his way, he would rather hang out with a small group of close friends.

Mac stopped typing on her computer, and he met her gaze, realizing he might not be so different from her.

She leaned forward, her black, silky hair falling across the collar of her navy blue dress shirt. "Are you ready for the job interview?"

He shrugged. "Yeah, I think so."

"Why aren't you more excited?"

"To be honest with you, I don't want to be an up front manager." He tapped the pen faster as a look of confusion crossed her face.

"Why not?"

"Working around all those people … It's not really my thing."

She snatched the pen from his hand and shoved it

back in the rotating container near her computer. "Most of my clients would love the opportunity to work at a store like Charger's. You're lucky your brother is willing to give you an interview."

Charlie rolled his eyes. Mac didn't know Daniel. "You assume my brother is being nice. He just wants me to have a job so I'll have enough money to move out of his house when my parole is over."

She tilted her head, studying him in a focused way that made him feel like she cared. "Don't you get along?"

He cracked his knuckles. "Not really."

"Is it because you went to prison?"

"No, we haven't gotten along in a while." He clenched his jaw. Daniel had never forgiven Charlie for ratting him out to their parents and getting him into trouble when they were in high school. His parents had been so fed up with Daniel's behavior they'd sent him to a boot camp.

"How come you aren't staying with your parents then? Your file shows they still live in Maple Valley."

"They do, but during the spring and summer they stay at their lake home. And now that they're retired, they travel a lot, so they aren't home much."

"Have you seen them since you got out?"

"Yeah." He rubbed the back of his neck. Both visits had been awkward. It was clear his parents didn't know what to say to him. They never brought up prison or parole, as if avoiding the topic somehow made his charges go away.

Mac rested her elbows on her desk, and her searching eyes brought heat pooling into his stomach. Her irises had a greenish tint, making them aquamarine, like the color of the sea. "How did it go?"

"Not so great." Charlie leaned back in his chair and crossed a bent leg above his knee. "Let's just say things have been different between us since I went to prison."

"Why?"

"Status is everything to them. Having a son who went to prison was the worst thing that could've happened to them."

Mac frowned. "I'm sure they're having a hard time, too. They probably miss their daughter-in-law." She said it quietly, not in the reprimanding way she'd talked to him before, but in a way that made it seem like she wanted him to see his parents' perspective.

"You're right. They probably do." He looked down at her desk, not willing to meet her gaze. "We all miss Ally."

"Have you visited her gravesite?"

His head jerked up. "No. Her parents didn't want me at the funeral."

"Where is she buried?"

"At Resting Haven Cemetery, right outside of town."

"That's not too far. You could take the bus there."

Sensing his hesitation, Mac tugged at the collar of her shirt. Dark blotches were spreading down her neck. "I think you should go."

He shook his head. He wasn't ready. Seeing Ally's grave would make her death final, and even though he'd come to grips with it, he couldn't bring himself to visit her at the cemetery yet.

"You need to have closure. You can't move on if you're still living in the past."

Heat pulsated in his veins. Mac was only trying to help, but she'd struck a nerve that gnawed at his insides. "Have *you* ever lost someone you love?"

"No, not exactly." She unfastened the top buttons on her shirt, tugging again.

"Then you have no idea what I need to do to have closure."

The color drained from her face, a stark contrast to the darkening crimson blotches on her neck. She picked up the coffee mug sitting on her desk and studied him, her eyes apologetic. "You're right. Will you at least think about what I said, though?"

His heart tugged unexpectedly. He hadn't meant to make her feel bad; he was only trying to be honest with her. "Yeah, I will."

"Thank you." She leaned forward and slid the paper toward him. The movement caused the unbuttoned top of her shirt to slide sideways, exposing her cleavage.

His eyes traveled to the bare skin around her neckline and roamed down to her shapely chest.

"Oh." Mac caught his glance and hurriedly fastened the buttons at the top of her shirt.

Charlie opened his mouth and closed it. "I, uh … "

She turned her chair toward her computer and typed on to the keyboard without looking at him. "I think that's enough for today."

Nodding, he stood and turned around, walking quickly out of Mac's office. What was wrong with him, staring at her chest? He missed his wife and he was lonely; that had to be it. He could never imagine looking at a woman the way he'd once looked at Ally.

CHARLIE'S THROAT WENT dry as he stood on the sidewalk, gazing at the tall brick house with green shutters. After thinking about Mac's advice, he realized she was right—he needed closure. He wasn't ready to visit Ally's grave yet, but there was one place that could bring him some sense of closure. Their old house.

Everything looked just like he remembered. A bay window protruded from the house, nearly touching the longest branches of an old oak tree. Cement steps ascended the steep incline of the front yard, surrounded by mulch and rust red flowers. A painted mailbox, not far from the driveway, was covered with hand-drawn vines and roses.

He stepped closer to the driveway and ran his fingers over the mailbox. It felt like yesterday when Ally had stood barefoot on the sidewalk with a paintbrush in hand. They'd just moved in and she wanted their mailbox to replicate the colorful art she'd hung up all over their house. She spent hours swirling reds, yellows, and greens across the plain black mailbox. If only he could watch her paint one more time, to see her face light up as she transformed plain and simple items into vibrant pieces full of life.

The front door swung open and a little boy and girl raced into the yard. The boy hopped into a tire swing hanging from the oak tree. "Swing me!"

Charlie dropped his hand from the mailbox as the girl pushed on the boy's feet, propelling him backward.

"Higher," the boy squealed.

The girl giggled and pushed the boy harder. Her braided pigtails swung across her shoulders, the summer yellow almost the same color as Ally's. His chest constricted. What would it have been like to have children with Ally? Or to come home from work and see their kids playing in the yard, waiting for him?

The girl ran toward the swing just as her brother leaned back and kicked his legs. His feet collided with the girl's chest. She stumbled and fell to the ground, landing on her hands and knees. Standing, she wiped the dirt off of her dress. The mud smeared deeper into the pale purple polka dots. "Look what you did! I'm telling Mom." She dashed toward the open door.

Charlie stepped back to leave as a woman with frizzy blond hair followed the girl out into the yard.

The woman strode up to the boy who swung innocently back and forth. "Did you kick your sister?"

"It was an accident, Mom."

The woman grabbed the rope attached to the tire swing. "Apologize to your sister." She listened to the apology and ushered the kids inside when she made eye contact with Charlie. "Oh, can I help you?"

He leaned back on his heels, sticking his hands in his pockets. "I, uh … This used to be my house."

"I've always wondered who lived here before us. We just moved to Maple Valley a few months ago." She pointed at the mailbox. "Are you an artist?"

"My wife is … " He cleared his throat. "I mean *was*."

"Oh." Her cheeks reddened. "Well, she was very good. I love the mural of the rain forest in the master bathroom. I couldn't bring myself to paint over it."

A smile tugged at his lips. "She painted that after we honeymooned in Brazil."

"Wow. That must have been some honeymoon."

"Yeah." Blinking back the moisture in his eyes, Charlie took another step back. "I better get going. I just wanted to see the house again."

"Would you like to come in?"

He ran a hand through his hair. "No, that's okay."

"Are you sure?"

He looked back at the home, his chest tightening. "Okay. For a minute."

Smiling, she walked up the driveway and held the door open for him.

Inside, he slipped out of his Doc Martens and scanned the living room. A large square rug sat in front of the marble fireplace. Even though it lay dormant now, he saw the fire flickering to life. Sparks sizzling as logs crackled apart. Flames lighting up the darkened living room, dancing across Ally's body as he kissed every inch of her soft, bare skin.

"Mom, we're hungry," said the little girl.

"I better fix them lunch." As the woman disappeared into the next room, he took one last look at the fireplace before following her into a large, industrial styled kitchen with a brick backsplash.

The boy and girl rolled on the wooden floor, tickling each other. The woman cleared her throat. "Stop playing and sit at the table to eat, please." Once the kids were seated at the center island, she looked over at him. "Would you like anything to eat?"

He shook his head as the woman set two plates on the counter and spread peanut butter across the bread.

He tried not to picture Ally in the kitchen, but her image materialized anyway. Ally standing in front of the island, humming country songs and swaying her hips as she cooked. Ally letting Jackson sit on a chair, laughing as he barked for more table scraps.

"This is yummy," the girl said as she bit into her sandwich, peanut butter smearing across her face. The ache in his chest returned, or maybe it had never left. Ally had wanted to have children right away, but he'd convinced her to wait. If he wouldn't have been so wrapped up in work, he could have been a dad by now.

"Do you want to see the rest of the house?"

He blinked. "Sorry, what?"

The woman repeated the question, her eyebrows furrowing with concern.

The kitchen walls closed in on him. He opened his mouth, gulping for air. "Uh, no. Thanks for the offer."

"Are you okay?"

He couldn't answer. His heart pounded in his chest, threatening to explode out of his rib cage. Coming here had been a mistake. A deluded dream. As if he could somehow make peace with the past.

A LIGHT RAIN bathed the grass and pitter-pattered against the glass-roof pergola. Charlie slipped his bare legs into the hot tub. Pressing a button, the jets roared to life. His tight muscles uncoiled beneath the warm, pressured water. This was exactly what he needed after his interview at Charger's Sporting Goods.

Daniel had offered him the job, and Mac would want him to take it. He understood her reasoning. It was a job. Maybe not the job he wanted, but it was something he could put on his resume.

If he took it, he could move up the corporate ladder and make his dad proud again. A year before the accident, his dad had sat him down in the big leather chair overseeing the store and said, *Son, you're doing a great job here. This could all be yours someday if you keep up the good work.*

Yellow and red watercolors streaked the sky as the fading sun descended below the horizon, bathing the professionally trimmed yard. Back then the prestige of owning the family business would've made his mouth water. Now it left him with the bitter aftertaste of sour milk.

Charger's reeked of his past, a time when work had consumed his life and taken away the nights he should have spent with Ally.

Cicadas chirped incessantly from the nearby woods as the back door opened and Daniel strolled out onto the porch. Dressed in his swimsuit, Daniel stepped into the hot tub, submerging into the bubbling water until it stopped at his shoulders. He looked at Charlie. "Have you made a decision yet?"

"Give me some time to think about it."

Daniel ran a hand through his short brown hair, disheveling the combed layers. "What is there to think about?"

"I'm not sure what I want to do."

Daniel scowled. "What you *want*? You need a job."

"I know." Charlie lifted his arms out of the water, resting them against the outside of the hot tub. "Just drop it for now."

"Whatever." Daniel looked away, his gaze resting on the woods, lost in thought. In the silence, Charlie braced himself for whatever his brother was about to say. Daniel hadn't let up since he had come home. Comments about how he'd ruined his future or little innuendos to remind him of his mistakes.

Still looking at the woods, Daniel spoke, "Remember when Mom and Dad first built this house and I started that big bonfire?"

"You mean the time when you almost started a forest fire?"

"I had the *bonfire* under control, but you never believe what I say."

"That's because you lied all the time."

"I wasn't lying when I said your brakes sounded bad." Daniel returned his gaze to Charlie. "Ally would still be alive if you had listened to me."

Charlie gritted his teeth. "I did. I made the appointment at Car Mech's."

"Some good that did. You should've had your brakes fixed right away, but of course you didn't. You didn't trust the mechanics because they were my friends."

"That's not true."

Daniel sneered. "Yes, it is. Just admit it: you looked down on my friends because they weren't like your uptight preppy friends who had nothing better to do than study or play golf at the country club."

He couldn't deny his brother's accusation. When they were younger, Daniel and his friends were constantly getting into trouble, causing their parents to tighten the strings on him, the youngest. It was hard to look up to any of them when they did nothing but create problems for him.

He clenched his fists so tightly his fingernails bit into his palms. "I don't want to talk about this anymore."

A glint of humor sparked in Daniel's dark brown eyes. "You're right. The past is the past, so we should bury it. Move on with our lives."

How dare Daniel say anything about moving on with their lives! It was easy for him to say, when everything had worked out better than he'd planned—owner of Charger's, married, and a child on the way. Charlie stood up so fast that the blood rushed out of his head, creating a dizzying effect.

He shook off the unsteadiness and towered above his brother, clenching his fists even tighter. He wasn't going to sit back and take it anymore. Pulling back his arm, he aimed for Daniel's cheek.

Daniel flinched, but his lips curled into a satisfied smirk. "What are you going to do? Fight me?"

Chapter 6

"I'M SO UPSET with Charlie." Mac slid into a rooted stance and alternated forceful kicks at her punching bag. "Maybe I should remove him from his brother's house. If he can't control his anger, he'll be back in prison in no time."

Jen pulled her red hair back into a ponytail and slipped on her gloves, positioning them in front of her chest. "Do you know what the argument was about?"

"When Charlie's brother called, he said it had something to do with the car accident. But it doesn't matter. He almost punched his brother."

"Almost being the key word." Jen turned to the side and kicked her bag, nearly falling over. "I wouldn't like living with my older sisters. Heck, I didn't when I was younger, either. We were too competitive."

"*You* were competitive?"

Jen flashed a smile, her light brown freckles crowding together on her pale cheeks. "When it came to guys we were very competitive."

"Now that I believe." Laughing, Mac swung a right hook, her fist pounding into the firm, sandy cushion of the punching bag. "Anyway, I need to figure out why he has anger issues."

"It probably has to do with his accident and losing his wife."

"I think that's part of it." Mac pursed her lips. "But he said he didn't want to talk about the accident, so it's hard to know for sure. It could have something to do with his family. They don't seem very supportive."

"Guys hate talking about personal stuff." Jen shook her head. "When I lived with my ex-boyfriend, his dad was diagnosed with ALS. It took me a solid month to get my ex to talk about it."

"Men are ridiculous. Can't live with them, can't live without them—except, I firmly believe you can live without them."

"You just say that because you're a workaholic who doesn't make time to date." Jen gave her a playful shove.

"Hey, you're supposed to hit the bag, not me." She hopped away from Jen to stand on the other side of her bag. She tilted her head and peered over at her friend. "I'd date someone who met my standards, and I'm not going to settle for anything less."

Jen stopped moving and set a hand on her hip. "Here we go again."

"We've talked about dating a lot, but not standards."

"Guess I wasn't asking you the right questions so spill." Excitement sparkled in Jen's green eyes as if she'd just discovered a hidden treasure.

She sighed. There was no use trying to get out of answering. Jen was relentless. "Someone who stays in shape, but not a guy who is obsessed with his body." Jordan's obsession with looking at himself in a mirror was enough to drive her crazy. "I'm not attracted to someone overly affectionate." Adam's public handholding and hugging had been way too embarrassing. "I don't want a guy who only cares about money." Like when Nathan showed up in a limo wearing an Armani suit on their first date.

She kicked at the punching bag. Nope, she wasn't in a rush to date Mr. Wrong so she could find Mr. Right. As if there were such a thing.

The kickboxing trainer passed by them, flexing his massive arm muscles. "Level up, ladies."

She bent low, balancing on one leg and jumped into the air, slamming her other leg into the punching bag.

"Show-off." Jen swung at her bag and waited for the trainer to pass by before she stopped to take a breath. "That kick isn't getting you off the hook. What if you're missing a good guy right in front of you?"

She gave Jen a knowing look. "Tucker is out of the question."

"But he's such a nice guy. He's cute, he's a police

officer … "

"Exactly. How can I be respected as a woman in law enforcement if I date other officers? I can't. Besides, most of them are friends and I can't look at them that way."

Jen winked. "Are you saying you'd consider dating Tucker if you weren't colleagues?"

She shrugged. "Maybe, but since we are, it's not worth considering."

"Well, it's obvious he's in love with you."

She shook her head. Loose strands of hair fell out of her ponytail, tickling her chin. "He's not in love with me."

"Oh yeah? Then why is he always spending time with you?" Jen's eyebrows rose up and down. "Think about it. He goes to kickboxing. It's not the manliest sport."

"Look. There are other guys in here."

"Guys with their girlfriends or wives," Jen corrected.

She followed Jen's gaze, realizing her friend was right. "Touché, but you're wrong about Tucker. There's no such thing as love."

"Of course there is. Why would I date if I didn't want to fall in love and get married?"

"Love is just an illusion to make people feel connected in relationships." As a child she'd hoped that it could exist. But she'd seen so much brokenness, so much pain—as a parole officer and growing up with an abusive dad—to believe it could be real.

Jen crossed her arms, unaware of the buried emotions Mac held within. "And you know so much about relationships? When was the last time you had a boyfriend?"

She stopped moving and steadied her punching bag. "That was uncalled for."

"Well, I'm offended. I can't imagine what you think of me when I go out on dates. You obviously think it's a waste of time."

Heat crept into her cheeks. She didn't consider dating a waste of time, but there were much more productive things to do, things that would lead to less heartbreak. "Don't take it personally. My views have nothing to do with you." It had more to do with her parents. If they didn't love her, then love couldn't possibly exist. At least, she wanted to believe that, because if she was wrong, it meant she was unlovable. And she definitely wasn't getting into *that* conversation with Jen. Her roommate wouldn't understand.

The trainer stood in front of the gym and cupped his hands in front of his mouth. "That's it for tonight. See you next week."

Pulling off her gloves, Jen reached for her water bottle, tipped her head back, and drank the whole thing. She screwed the cap back on and dabbed at her wet lips with her manicured fingers. "What happened? Did you date some guy who told you he loved you and then cheated on you?"

"No, that's not it at all."

Walking through the warm gymnasium, Jen reached for Mac's arm and squeezed it. "All right, fine. You don't have to tell me who hurt you, but when you find the right guy, you'll realize that love is possible. And you deserve to know what it feels like."

"Look, that's a nice thought, but … "

Jen opened the door to the locker room, allowing Mac to pass through. "Believe what you want, my dear. I can have enough faith for the both of us."

She walked to her locker and opened it, swinging the metal door between them. Jen was such a hopeless romantic. But as for her, *she* wasn't waiting around for some fairy-tale romance. And she definitely wasn't looking for Prince Charming to show up and sweep her off her feet.

DOORBELLS JINGLED AS Mac walked into Val's Diner. The smell of coffee, syrup, and pancakes swirled through the restaurant. Inhaling the enticing aromas, she scanned the crowded diner for Jen and Tucker.

Behind the counter, Valerie poured coffee into the mayor's mug. The waitress's black, shiny hair was styled high into an afro, making her appear even taller than normal. She glanced up at Mac, her loud voice carrying above the lively chatter. “Want the usual?”

She nodded at Valerie as Tucker caught her attention from one of the tables in the middle of the restaurant. Heading toward them, she maneuvered through the tightly packed diner, stopping midstride. Charlie sat at a nearby booth, eating steak and eggs. She immediately ran through a list of everything she wanted to say to him—mostly different versions of *What the heck were you thinking almost punching your brother?*

But when his eyes met hers, she forgot everything she wanted to say, and all she could do was stare. His athletic T-shirt clung to his sculpted shoulders and the sleeves could barely contain his well-defined arms.

Moving closer, she waved, then silently cursed inside her head for the awkward gesture. Why did she feel so rattled around him? Something was seriously wrong with her. She needed to get a grip.

Her gaze lowered to Charlie’s plate. He had barely touched his food. The steak was cut into pieces, but instead of eating it, he was moving the food around on his plate with a fork.

“Morning,” he said.

“Same to you.” She stopped beside his table, noticing the dark circles shadowed beneath his heavily lidded eyes. Stubble ran from his square jawline to his cheeks. She wanted to ask him what was wrong, but then thought better of it. "How's your breakfast?"

"Fine."

"You haven't eaten much of it."

"I didn't come here for the food. I just needed a place to think."

"And you chose Val's Diner?"

"Noise helps me think."

"Oh." She twisted her lips, trying to figure out what he needed to think about, then remembering he'd had the interview a few days ago. "Did you get offered the position at Charger's?"

"Yeah."

Across the room, she caught Jen's attention and held up her pointer finger, mouthing, "one minute." Jen gave a thumbs-up and Mac slipped into the booth across from Charlie. "Are you going to take it?" she asked.

"I don't know."

"Just remember, any job is a step in the right direction. You don't have to work at Charger's forever." When he didn't respond right away, she shifted in the booth.

Swallowing a bite, the corner of his mouth curled up to one side as he gestured with his fork. "Don't worry; I'll apply to hundreds of other companies while I make my decision."

She rolled her eyes. "Hundreds, huh? I don't think there are that many openings in this small town."

He smirked. "Yup, hundreds, and they're all offering hiring bonuses and company cars."

She shook her head. His sarcasm could be covering up for insecurity, but at least he was enjoying the banter.

Valerie set a steaming cup of coffee in front of Mac before hustling away.

Grabbing the mug, she scooted out from the booth. If she sat with Charlie too long, this could look like a date, warranting an investigation by Warren. "I better get going. My friends are waiting."

"Hold on." Charlie dropped his fork and reached out, touching her hand. The intensity of his brown eyes stole the air from her lungs. "Before you go, can I ask you a question?"

She glanced at Jen and Tucker across the diner, slipping her hand out of Charlie's grasp. Ignoring her friends' curious looks, she met his gaze. "What is it?"

"Are you going to prolong my parole if I don't take the job?"

She slid back to the middle of the booth, sitting directly across from him. "Why don't you want the job? Does this have something to do with your brother?"

"Yes and no." Picking up the saltshaker, he tossed it from hand to hand, sliding it across the table. "I worked a lot of extra hours at Charger's. Time I should've spent at home with Ally. If I work there again, that's all I'd be able to think about."

What was she supposed to say to that? *I feel bad for you? I'm sorry you miss Ally?* She couldn't say that to the man who'd played a key role in his wife's death.

He turned his head toward the window, a faraway look in his eyes. Pinching the bridge of his nose, he said, "Ally didn't deserve to die."

A lump formed in her throat as a seed of compassion lodged there. "I know you said you don't want to talk about it, but what happened that night?"

Charlie stopped moving the saltshaker. "It's not something I like to talk about."

"I think you have a lot of built up anger. If you don't talk to someone, I'm worried you'll do something you regret."

They exchanged a long glance as Charlie sighed and leaned back, a defeated expression crossing his face. "Maybe you're right."

Mac lifted the coffee mug to her lips, peering at Charlie over the rim as she waited for him to start. She sat with her back straight against the booth, unable to relax. Even though she was starting to like him, she wasn't so sure she could suppress her own memories of his accident, and the bitterness that stemmed from that night.

His lips parted before the words came tumbling out. "It was our anniversary and we were running late for our dinner reservations at Cozy Cosinos." His Adam's apple bobbed up and down. “It took me months to get those reservations and I didn’t want to lose our spot. That’s why I was speeding so fast.”

“But there was a snowstorm. Weren’t you worried about getting into an accident?” she asked quietly.

“No, I always drove fast, but that night I was speeding even faster than normal. Ally got upset with me though, so I tried to slow down, but my brakes wouldn’t work and I ran the red light.” He ran his thumb over the top of the saltshaker. “A car hit the passenger side of my BMW. Ally was gone before I could tell her how much I loved her.”

Mac stiffened. Tucker’s squad car had been right behind Charlie’s BMW at the stoplight. She’d seen his sports car shooting through the red light just as the white van smashed into the passenger side, spinning the BMW around in circles. A woman’s screams—surely Ally’s—had pierced through the frigid night, then suddenly disappeared.

She bit her lip to stop a grimace from forming. “I’m glad your wife passed quickly. She probably didn’t feel much pain.”

“Ally shouldn’t have had to feel any pain, not one second of it.” He pressed his thumb harder across the saltshaker, knocking it over. Salt trickled onto the table. “It should have been me. I should’ve died.”

Before meeting Charlie, she would’ve agreed. But

now, as she sat across the table from him, pain etched across his face, she couldn't think that way at all. "But you didn't die," she said in a soft tone.

"I don't know if I can move on." He looked so big as he rested his forearms on the table, his biceps chiseled with muscle, but when he frowned, his face was as vulnerable as a child's. She suddenly felt the itch to comfort him and run her hands over those muscular arms. "Don't you think Ally would want you to move on?"

He slunk back against the booth, his handsome face contorted in sorrow. "Yeah, I do, but … It's easier said than done."

"I think you can." She almost reached across the table to hold his hands. To make him feel better, if only for a moment. Resisting the urge, she tightly wrapped her hands around her mug, her knuckles turning white. "You've applied for very difficult jobs, which shows me that you're willing to try."

"You sound like a counselor."

She shook her head. "I'm definitely not a counselor. I'm not patient enough."

"Sounds familiar." A sad smile flickered across his face as he wiped the salt from the table into the palm of his hand. "Trust me: one thing I learned in prison is that everybody needs more patience."

"You're admitting you learned something in prison?"

He chucked softly. "Yeah, I guess I am."

Her chest constricted. The full cost of the accident had become crystal clear. Ally wasn't the only one who had lost her future when she died. Charlie had lost his, too.

But she couldn't help noticing he'd never mentioned anything about drinking. Was it possible he'd been telling the truth?

It didn't seem plausible.

The thought gave her a stab of disappointment. Somehow in the last few weeks she'd really started to like him.

CHARLIE SAT UP in bed, taking deep, rapid breaths. His eyelids felt heavy, but he kept them open. If he fell asleep too quickly, he'd fall back into the nightmare, the one where he relived the accident over and over again.

He shifted from his back to his side. Beside him, Jackson yawned and stretched his limbs, pressing his paws against Charlie's bare chest. He scratched Jackson's stomach, the familiar ache of Ally's absence returning with vigor.

Light from the moon pierced through the skylight, illuminating the bedroom. Blinking, he glanced around the cluttered room, his stomach knotting. Weeks ago, his parents had brought over the crates they'd kept while he was in prison. The crates still remained unopened. The ghosts of his past lived in those boxes. If he looked through them, he'd see some of Ally's things—painful reminders of what used to be.

And yet, he needed to wash away the guilty residue of the nightmare. His heart ached to see the keepsakes, to remember Ally alive, not lifeless in his arms.

Rolling off the side of the bed, he walked across the room, turned on the light, and sat on the floor. He crossed his legs and pulled a crate toward him.

He carefully lifted each item out of the container and studied them: their wedding album from Brazil, a receipt from Candy Galore, a You're the Best Teacher medal. For the first time since Ally's death, he allowed himself to remember. Taking her out for ice cream on their first date. Carrying her into the bedroom on their wedding night. Watching her face light up when she talked about her students. Kissing her at the most random moments. The memories washed over him, drowning and refreshing him all at once. He opened one crate after the next, feeling the full impact of his love, happiness, and loss.

In the last box, he found an oil-based painting Ally had given him for Christmas, their last holiday together.

He slumped against the wall, studying the canvas. It depicted an afternoon when they had built a snowman in their front yard. In the painting, snowflakes fell from the sky, landing on their thick, puffy coats as he threw a snowball at her and Jackson jumped into the air, trying to eat it.

He clutched the canvas to his chest. Ally had loved to paint. Once they had kids, she'd planned on resigning from teaching to start her career as an artist. He'd always admired her for that choice because he could never imagine leaving a secure, well-respected job. There were too many risks involved, although with his job at Charger's, he hadn't worried about supporting their family in case she never made any money.

Bringing the canvas away from his chest, he stared at the carefully crafted details. Every minute detail exuded all the joy that Ally had breathed into her work. He blinked away tears. Ally would've been happy painting, pursuing her dream, and being a stay-at-home mom, but she'd never had the chance.

His finger trailed across the painting, lingering over Ally's smile. Unlike her, he'd never been passionate about his job, no matter how much his dad and brother assumed he was. Charger's was a place to work, to make money, to make his dad proud.

He closed his eyes, imagining Ally with a paintbrush in hand, happily singing to a country song on the radio. *What should I do about Charger's, Ally? Should I take the job?*

A warm, tingling sensation traveled through him as the answer came to him as clear and vivid as the painting she'd made for him.

Chapter 7

DANIEL STOOD IN front of the open window in his office, overlooking downtown Maple Valley. He lit the tip of a cigarette, inhaling. The nicotine washed through his body but did little to ease his mind. Why hadn't Charlie made a decision yet? His brother had to be toying with him. That had to be it. Charlie had always wanted to work at Charger's. In fact, he'd wanted to be the owner.

Exhaling, the smoke spiraled around his face. At least Charlie had no idea that their dad had planned on asking him to be the owner instead of Daniel. Dad never got the chance to tell Charlie. The car accident happened just days after Dad's retirement announcement and without Charlie in the picture, Daniel was given the opportunity to show their dad that he could run the business. That was all he'd needed to prove he had what it took.

The secretary knocked on the door and opened it a crack. "Charlie's on line two."

"Got it." As the door clicked shut, he waved at the clouding smoke and threw his cigarette out the open window. He plopped into his big leather chair and reached for the phone. "What's it going to be?"

"I don't want the job." Charlie's voice came through loud and clear.

But there was no way he meant it. He had to be messing around. Daniel struggled to keep his tone even. "You're turning down my offer?"

"I'd like to work somewhere else."

"You arrogant prick." With his free hand, Daniel pounded his fist on the desk. "And to think I was doing you a favor."

"I don't need you to do me any favors."

His brother was making a big mistake. "You're on parole. How can you get a decent job?"

A few seconds went by before his brother answered. "I don't know yet."

Charlie had lost his common sense. Of all the stupid, selfish things he could do, this would be the worst. "Don't ever step foot in this store again."

"I—"

That was it. He didn't need more excuses from his brother. Daniel threw his phone at the nearest wall, knocking down a picture of him and his dad. The frame broke into pieces, and glass splattered across the carpet near his desk.

He stood and paced back and forth across the office with his hands on his head. This was all MacKenna Christensen's fault. She was the one who had called and asked him to give Charlie an interview. After thinking about it, he'd decided it was a good idea. If Charlie worked at Charger's, Daniel would have more opportunities to get under his brother's skin. Hopefully, he could provoke Charlie enough to start a fight. And when that happened, his brother would get sent back to prison and be out of his life once again. Now that he'd experienced a world without his brother, he didn't want to go back to the way it had once been.

He kicked at the broken frame. But Charlie hadn't taken the job and now Daniel looked like a fool. All because of MacKenna Christensen. That was the last time he'd play by her rules.

MAC LEANED BACK against the sofa in Daniel's sunroom and extended her legs to the floor, crossing her ankles. The afternoon sun cascaded through the windows, warming the bare skin below her knee-length skirt. Holding a straw to her lips, she sipped her iced coffee and peered at Charlie. "Where did you run?"

"Angel's Creek Park." He sat on the wood floor, his legs sprawled out in opposite directions as he stretched his arms toward his left foot. Sweat glistened across his forehead, dripped down his face, and bled through his light blue T-shirt.

"It's nice going somewhere, instead of running in a circle around the prison yard." He switched directions with his arms. The back of his shirt lifted, exposing hard, lean muscles.

She wondered what it would feel like to run her hands up and down his back. But before her thoughts could go any further, she averted her gaze and set her coffee on an end table. "Sometimes I walk Bruno on that trail. It's best in the morning, before the bugs are out, but I usually don't wake up that early. Six is early enough for me, and then it takes about two cups of coffee to make me human. Otherwise, you run into a grouchy grizzly bear."

"A grizzly bear, huh? Is that why most of our meetings are in the afternoon?"

"Now you know my secret." She looked back at Charlie, wishing she could cover her eyes with her hand. He stood up, lifting the back of his tennis shoes, then lowering them. His calf muscles bulged every time he rose an inch higher.

Heat pooled low into her stomach and she forced herself to look away, opening her briefcase and digging out her laptop. "How's the job search going?"

"Besides my brother, I haven't heard back from anyone." He sat back down on the floor, pulling his knees up to his chest. Jackson, who had been sleeping on one of the sofas, jumped off and lay beside him, resting his head on top of Charlie's foot. "This is harder than I thought it would be."

"Can you think of anywhere in Maple Valley you'd consider applying?"

"No."

"You can't think of *one* place?"

"You don't understand." For a brief moment, Charlie lowered his gaze. "People in Maple Valley don't want to see me. Not after … Well, you know."

"You might be surprised to find that people aren't as mad at you as you think. Maybe they're more upset at the situation." Like she had been.

"Maybe."

"And to be honest with you, it sounds like the other way around. *You* don't want to see them."

Charlie glanced out the open window at his brother's backyard, a faraway look in his eyes.

"You have to face everyone at some point."

He ran a hand over Jackson's fur.

She opened her laptop, running through a list of possible businesses in her head. "What about the Canine Palace?"

Turning to face her, his eyebrows creased together. "I've never heard of it."

"Do you remember Ray Meyers, the high school football coach?"

"Yeah."

"He retired and opened the store a few years ago. It's a cute little shop for dogs."

"What kind of position could I have there?"

"Ray runs the store by himself." Mac shrugged. "Maybe you could convince him to hire you as an accountant."

Charlie scratched behind Jackson's ears, seeming to consider her suggestion. "I'll give it a try."

"Awesome." She gave him a tentative smile. Once a month she took Bruno to the Canine Palace to get his nails clipped and to get a thorough wash. She couldn't resist giving someone like Ray Meyers business. He was the heart and soul of this town. The old football coach everyone loved and adored. The storeowner who gave discounts to anyone who put money in a fund to help veterans find jobs. No one would be a better boss than Ray. Hopefully, he would hire Charlie. Time was running out and he needed a job or he'd go back to prison.

Standing up, Charlie refilled his empty glass with a pitcher of water sitting on an end table. "I'll talk to Ray tomorrow." Despite his reluctance to apply, his tone sounded pleasant, relieved even. Maybe just the simple act of making a decision was enough to lessen his worries.

She typed his goal into her laptop. *Get hired at the Canine Palace.*

He strolled over to stand beside the sofa and leaned over her shoulder, cupping his hands over his knees. "Is that my file?"

His minty breath glided across her cheek, sending shivers up and down her arms. "We uh … we have a database full of information about our clients."

"That's a little weird," he said, his voice light. "I hope my favorite foods and shows aren't listed. That would be really creepy."

"Yes, it would." She hid her smile. "I guess you'll just have to give me a list of your favorite things."

"Is that my next homework assignment?" Charlie walked to the other sofa and sat down on top of the flowery cushions. He grinned at her, a cute dimple appearing on his chin.

"Yes, of course. It's very important that you do it right away."

A warm breeze blew through the sunroom, picking up the scent of Charlie's cologne. How could a guy smell that good after running? Unexpected warmth crept into her cheeks. She flipped her laptop closed and slid it in her briefcase. "Well … "

Charlie cracked his knuckles and tapped his bare foot on the wood floor, bouncing his leg and creating a rhythmic beat.

"We'll meet next week at … " She stopped talking. Tapping filled the lull of silence. "Why are you doing that?"

"Doing what?"

"You're bouncing your leg."

Charlie stopped moving. He bent his leg and crossed it over his knee. "Sorry."

"Have you always had trouble staying still? I've noticed how often you tap your foot, or bounce your leg, or crack your knuckles."

He shrugged. "Yeah, I guess so. I have a lot of built up energy."

"Why?"

Charlie pressed his knuckles against his other hand, but stopped before they cracked. A guilty smile spread across his face like a child caught with his hand in the cookie jar. "It happens when I'm cooped up in one place for too long. I think that's why I used to drive so fast. It was such a rush."

She should stop asking questions, apologize for being nosy, and leave. But the more he opened up, the more she wanted to know. "What else helps?"

"Being outside, running or walking. When I worked at Charger's, I'd walk around the store to burn off the extra energy." He chuckled. "One of the cashiers thought I had a crush on him because I walked by his register so often."

She laughed. "You're one of a kind."

Smiling, he winked at her, sending her heart into overdrive. "I'm going to take that as a compliment," he said.

"Don't be so conceited." She tried to sound sassy, but a wide grin spread across her face.

CHARLIE SLID HIS sandals across the *Wipe Your Paws* mat at the front entrance of the Canine Palace. Iced frosting and wet dog hair perfumed the small, decorated shop. Jackson darted to the treat counter, his nose in the air.

"Welcome to the kingdom for dogs." Ray Meyers stepped out of the backroom dressed in jeans and an orange T-shirt with a white paw printed on the breast pocket. He pushed his thick glasses higher on his nose and smoothed a wild strand of gray hair sticking out from his head. Glancing at Charlie, recognition spread across his weathered face. "I wondered if you'd stop by. I've seen you walking that dog around town."

Charlie withheld a sigh. Nothing could get past anyone in this small place. He couldn't get out of here fast enough. As soon as parole was over, he'd be gone for good.

Stepping farther into the store, he noticed Ray was

still looking at him, waiting for a response. "MacKenna Christensen just told me about this place."

"MacKenna, huh? Is she your parole officer?"

"Yeah."

"Lucky you. She's a sweetheart."

Charlie nodded politely. He wouldn't exactly call her a sweetheart, but she was loosening up and becoming someone he enjoyed spending time with. Actually, she was the only person he enjoyed spending time with lately.

"Well, take a look around. Let me know if you have any questions."

"Okay, thanks." Charlie followed Jackson around the store. It was small, no bigger than the size of a living room. A variety of dog toys hung from a long wall directly across from the entrance. Off to one side was a grooming station and on the other side was a glass counter filled with dog treats. Birthday cakes, cookies, and frosted bones lined the shelves like pastries in a bakery.

He walked over to the glass counter, his eyes widening. "Do you make all these?"

Ray hooked his thumbs in his jean pockets. "Yeah. I bake everything from scratch. I came up with these recipes a few years ago and had my daughter sell them at some of the football games. People kept asking for more, so that's when I decided to open this shop."

"Wow, that's impressive." Leaning over the top of the counter, he surveyed the rest of the treats, finding hotdogs, burgers, and fries. He picked up a bag of fries and held them by his nose, inhaling a scent similar to McDonald's.

Jackson jumped on his hind legs and Ray crouched down next to him. "What's your dog's name?"

"Jackson."

"Jack Russell's are a great breed. Very smart dogs." The old man scratched behind Jackson's ears as the dog licked Ray's white beard. "I'm sure he'd love those fries."

Charlie grabbed the fries and a few frosted cookies. He had to find a way to change the conversation and focus on possible job openings. "I'll buy the fries, the cookies, and … " He looked around the rest of the quaint store, then strolled over to the wall of toys. He grabbed a pink pig, squeezing it. The pig squealed. Jackson dashed over and jumped into the air, trying to bite the toy. "And this pig."

"Perfect choices." Ray took the items and set them on a counter with *Bone Appetit* scrolled across the top. He dropped them into a small paper bag and typed the prices into the register. "Your total is $10.50."

Pushing back his shoulders, he cleared his throat. "Do you need an accountant?"

"I do all the accounting around here."

"Oh." His shoulders lowered.

Ray took off his Coke-bottle glasses, cleaning the lenses with the bottom of his T-shirt. "I do have an opening, though."

"What is it?"

"A dog walker. I can never keep the position filled." Ray slipped the glasses back on his nose, his eyes assessing Charlie's face as if he'd asked Ray to check for food stuck in his teeth. "Know why?"

"Why?"

"Because no one wants to clean up poop." The old man lightly slapped his palm on the counter. "I think we all need to clean up a little poop every now and then. Brings humility, which brings wisdom."

"Sure, if you say so." Charlie chuckled. "Walk dogs, pick up poop ... What else do I need to know about the job?"

Ray rested his elbows above the counter. "I need someone who can work five days a week, six hours a day. It's minimum wage. There's a long trail nearby that runs along the river. The dogs love to go out there and follow scents. That's the best place to walk them."

Charlie shifted his weight from one foot to the other. The job had its perks. He could be outside, by the river. He'd be surrounded by dogs and could probably bring Jackson to work with him. He withheld a smile. Mac would be pleased, which could only mean better odds of completing parole.

He suddenly felt an unexpected pinch of disappointment. As much as he wanted parole to be over, he wasn't quite sure he wanted his time with Mac to end. Since he'd moved home, he'd spent a lot of time with her. It was mostly his fault, not calling up his old friends to hang out, but he'd been too afraid they wouldn't answer, or worse, they'd tell him no. It was better not knowing if he still had friends.

Ray cleared his throat. "You can stop considering whether you want the job. I won't hire you."

Charlie crossed his arms. He should have known. Ray didn't want to hire him because of his criminal record. He was just like everybody else.

"You deserve better."

"Huh?"

"I can't believe you were put behind bars. Negligence shouldn't result in prison time." Ray shook his head. "I don't want you settling for a job here."

His lips parted. Had he heard the old man correctly? "But you need a dog walker."

"Oh well."

"You just told me a few minutes ago that people need to pick up poop."

"You forgot the rest of it. People need to pick up poop because it brings them wisdom. You already have wisdom." Ray's eyes twinkled behind his glasses.

"How can you tell?"

The old man gave him a quirky smile. "I'm not hiring you."

"Look, I don't know if anyone else *will* hire me. I've applied to other places already and I've only had one interview." He ran a hand through his hair. "What if you hired me, just for a while? I'll work hard and I'm good with dogs."

"Good. That's settled."

"What's settled?"

"You want the job."

"Yes, that's what I just said." Never had he imagined becoming a dog walker, but it would do for now. And working for someone as quirky as Ray would be interesting. No doubt there would be very few dull moments, if any. He pressed his fist against the counter. "What do you say? Do I have the job or not?"

Chapter 8

THE DOOR SWOOSHED shut, causing the string of bells hanging from the doorway to chime their welcoming jingle. Bruno ran out of the grooming station and Mac crouched down, pressing her nose against his freshly shampooed fur. "He smells great."

Ray grabbed Bruno's leash from the grooming station, handing it over to her. "You know, I wouldn't have to wash Bruno so often if you didn't let him swim in the dirty river water."

"Maybe I want an excuse to see you."

"Is that why you sent Mr. Grimm to work for me?" Ray eyed Charlie, who stood at the front register with a pile of paperwork on the counter. At the mention of his name, Charlie turned around, dressed in cargo shorts and a button-down shirt rolled up to his elbows.

Her heart lurched. She hadn't expected him to be here. "I thought you started next week."

"I do, but I came in to fill out tax forms."

"Oh." Her cheeks flushed as she tugged at her tight

jean shorts, pulling them down a little lower on her thighs. *Dang it.* If she had known he would be here, she would've worn something else, something a little less revealing.

He turned back to his paperwork, and she could've sworn she'd seen a slight smile playing on his lips.

With Charlie's attention on his forms, she took the opportunity to pull her tank top higher. She wasn't used to seeing clients in Maple Valley. The Department of Corrections served one entire judicial district in Iowa, so most clients lived in other towns or cities.

She finished adjusting her shirt and focused her attention on Ray, who was giving her a curious look. "You caught me," she said, finally answering his question. "I just wanted another excuse to see you."

"You sure know how to melt an old man's heart." Ray put a tan, wrinkled hand over his chest. "But you should save those winks for Tucker. I heard you had dinner with him at Val's Diner last week. You two an item?"

Rolling her eyes, she clicked the leash on to Bruno's collar and stood. "I'm not getting into that with you, Ray Meyers."

He lifted his hands in innocence. "Just asking."

She glanced at Charlie. Had he heard Ray's comment? With his back to her, it was impossible to tell. Hopefully, he hadn't.

Being single in a small town gave the older residents something to talk about. They were always asking about her dating life, and most days she didn't mind. They meant well. But clients didn't need to hear about her personal life, especially Charlie. Unlike other offenders, he grew up in a stable home with two parents in a well-off neighborhood. His upbringing made her look at him differently. If he hadn't committed a crime, he was someone she would consider dating.

The thought left her frozen for a moment. *Holy cow.* Her feelings for Charlie had really changed. And now that they had, she had the sinking feeling this guy could get her into serious trouble.

Looking away from him, she took her phone out of her purse and clicked on the calendar. "While I'm here, I'd like to set up Bruno's next appointment."

"I can set it up for you." Charlie walked around the counter and reached for the schedule book, flipping through the pages.

She bit her bottom lip. If he had heard her request, then he'd surely overheard Ray's comment about Tucker. She bit the inside of her cheek.

Charlie leaned over the counter and rested his elbows over the book, giving her a lopsided grin. He eyed her from head to toe, and her stomach did a little flip-flop. As his gaze traveled back to her face, she couldn't look away. She could get lost in those caramel brown eyes of his.

His grin never faded. "You don't need to be embarrassed."

"I'm not." She tucked a strand of hair behind her ear and took a step back, putting more space between them. Her heart was beating too loud, too fast.

He gave her a knowing look, his left eyebrow arching. She was pretty sure he was being playful, but on a handsome face like his, it just looked sexy. "Even a parole officer has to have a life outside of work, right?"

She glanced down at the open page, cursing at herself. *Stupid, stupid, stupid. He's a client. Get a hold of yourself.* Swallowing the lump in her throat, she suggested a date and time.

"Perfect." He penciled her in and shut the book.

The dog-themed clock struck nine o'clock with a loud bark.

Startled, Mac jumped and Charlie gave a low chuckle.

"Okay kids, I'm closing up for the night." Ray reached for a broom and started sweeping the grooming station. "It's time to skedaddle."

Charlie walked around the front counter, brushing past her, and the air felt like it was being sucked from the room. He crossed through the small store, handing Ray his paperwork. "Do you want help closing?"

"No, I'll do it." Wheezing, Ray bent over and

scooped Bruno's dog hair into the dustpan. "You're young. Get out of here and enjoy your weekend." He swiped the broom through the air, toward the door, kicking them out.

"Okay, okay. We get the picture." Charlie waved at Ray and held the door open for her and Bruno.

Her heart swelled. What a gentleman to hold the door for her. As she stepped out of the store, the streetlamps turned on, illuminating the old brick road. She slipped her free hand inside the pocket of her shorts, trying to appear more at ease than she actually felt. "I'll see you next Wednesday."

"Perfect. See you then." He sent her another playful grin and leaned back on his heels. "Unless you decide to check on me before that."

She put her hand on her hip. "I was *not* checking up on you. Bruno had an appointment."

"Uh-huh, sure. Whatever you say."

She opened her mouth to respond, but Charlie turned around and headed up the street. Was he flirting with her? If so, he was definitely overstepping boundaries.

Part of her hoped she wasn't just imagining it.

Guilt sank like a heavy anchor in her stomach. She shouldn't wish such a thing.

She led Bruno a few feet down the sidewalk and picked him up, lifting him into the passenger's seat of her truck.

"Charlie!" a loud voice called from the sidewalk.

Mac turned around, the truck door squeaking shut behind her.

Hannah waddled toward Charlie and stopped beneath a streetlamp. "I need to talk to you."

"What's up?" he asked.

Hannah wore a serious expression. "Don't take the job at the Canine Palace."

Mac stepped closer, standing between her truck and a parked Jeep. Why would Hannah want Charlie to turn down a job? After talking to her before some of Charlie's parole meetings, it seemed like she had his best interest at heart.

Charlie set his hand on Hannah's shoulder. "I'm not going to change my mind. I want to work at the Canine Palace."

"Don't you want to smooth things over with Daniel?"

Mac leaned against the hood of her truck with no intention of leaving. Not if the conversation could give her insight into Charlie and Daniel's relationship.

He slid his hand into his pocket and frowned at Hannah. "It's not that simple."

"I know, but—" She stopped short.

An attractive man with dark brown hair and a goatee strode down the sidewalk, scowling. "What are you two doing together?"

Hannah took a step away from Charlie. "I was just trying to tell him that he should work at Charger's."

The man set a cigarette in his mouth, touching the tip with his lighter. A puff of smoke spiraled around his face. Letting the cigarette dangle from his lips, he waved at the smoke with his hand. "Don't bother. You can't help people who don't want help."

Mac looked from Charlie to the man beside him. Same brown eyes. Same square jawline. Same dark hair. The guy must be Charlie's older brother. She'd hoped to meet Daniel by now, but he'd always been working at Charger's during Charlie's house meetings.

Charlie crossed his arms. "I don't need your help. I can figure out my life on my own."

"See what I mean?" Daniel looked at Hannah. "He thinks he's too good for *us*."

Mac's eyes widened. What was Daniel's problem?

Turning completely away from Charlie, Daniel reached for Hannah's hand. "Let's go to dinner. We don't need anyone seeing us with him." He looked up and down the sidewalk.

She ducked down, the blood draining from her face. Hopefully, Daniel hadn't seen her. This conversation had turned into way more than she'd bargained for. Why was Daniel treating Charlie so harshly? He was the one who'd agreed to let Charlie live at his house, after all.

She'd have to talk to Warren about Daniel's demeaning attitude.

"Have a nice dinner." The sarcastic voice belonged to Charlie.

She stayed still, listening to their receding footsteps. Maybe Daniel was causing problems for Charlie instead of the other way around. She had to find out for sure. A parolee's home environment could significantly affect his progress. Doing a curfew check would be the best way to catch Daniel at home.

Buzzing vibrations pulsated inside her purse. She pulled out her cell phone, clutching it between her ear and shoulder as she opened her truck and hopped inside. "This is MacKenna."

"Hi, this is James from the CDC. I'm calling to let you know your mom is leaving tomorrow morning. She's refusing further treatment."

"Is there any way you can make her stay?"

"I'm sorry. I can't hold a patient against her will." James sighed into the receiver. "I shouldn't have called, but I wanted to tell you—we found several cuts and bruises on Lynn's arms and legs and she's claiming to have fallen down the stairs before she arrived here."

"I know where they came from," she said quietly.

"Then hopefully you can convince her to come back."

"I'll try." She tossed her phone back into her purse

and slammed the truck door shut. Lynn had so much life left in her if she would just leave Jack. Somehow, she needed to convince Lynn of that, no matter how impossible it seemed. And right now, it felt really impossible. Groaning, she leaned forward, slumping against the steering wheel like a wilting flower.

"LYNN?" MAC KNOCKED on the door to her parents' apartment. No answer. She knocked again.

The door opened and an eye peeked through the crack. "What do you want?" Lynn's raspy voice slurred the question.

Mac glanced down at her watch, frowning. It wasn't even noon yet. She held up a plastic container of apple pie from Val's Diner. "I brought you pie."

A loud sigh escaped from inside the apartment as the door opened. She stepped inside. A rancid smell blanketed the room, stinging her nostrils. She tried not to gag and walked into the kitchen, setting the pie on a folding table. A pile of dirty dishes overflowed above the sink and across the countertop. An open bag of garbage sat on the faded linoleum.

Lynn walked in behind her, swaying. She leaned her bony hips against the chipped cabinets. "You can't stay long," she whispered.

"Why not?"

"Your dad is sleeping. If you wake him up, he'll be pissed."

Her stomach knotted as she tiptoed into the living room, a familiar scene from her childhood displayed on the floor. Beer cans littered the shag carpet. A jagged crack ran down the middle of a large box TV. An air mattress lay in the middle of the room with her dad passed out. His rhythmic snoring filled the mostly empty space.

She turned back to her mom, keeping her voice quiet. No way would she risk waking her dad. He'd surely take it out on her mom later. "Why did you leave the treatment center?"

Lynn crossed her arms, her body so frail that it looked like she was hugging herself. "I didn't want to be there anymore."

She scanned her mom's face and arms, searching for new cuts and bruises. A vibrant black and blue mark extended from Lynn's elbow and ran up her sleeve. She tore her eyes away from the bruise and glanced up at her mom's face. "Please leave Jack."

"No."

Her shoulders sagged. Days like today made her wish she had a boyfriend to help reason with her mom. If there were two of them, maybe Lynn would listen. Most of the time, it didn't bother her to be single, but how good would it feel to have someone hold her and tell her that Lynn would be okay?

Her mom staggered into the living room, sitting gently on the air mattress. She almost barrel-rolled onto the floor as she glanced at Mac with bloodshot eyes. "Get out of here."

Expelling a heavy breath, she trudged toward the door.

Her dad let out a deep cough, and she stopped midstride, turning around. He coughed again, followed by incessant choking. Her mom sat up straight, her back erect as she shook Jack by the shoulders. "Wake up."

His eyes remained closed as vomit trickled down his chin. Keeping her gaze locked on Jack, Lynn pushed off the mattress and pressed her hands against her cheeks. "This can't be happening."

A gurgling sound bubbled up from her dad's throat. Her mom's bloodshot eyes grew wide as she shot a look at Mac. "Call 9-1-1."

She froze. Did she want Jack to wake up? Her mom would be safer with him gone. The mattress shook as his body started convulsing. She couldn't just let him die. She yanked out her cell phone, her hands shaking as she dialed the numbers.

Chapter 9

USING THE STONE encased fire pit for light, Charlie shuffled a deck of cards. One by one, he laid the cards on the patio table, arranging them for a game of solitaire.

Beside him, Hannah reached for a bag of potato chips. "You should ask Mac to stay, then we could all play a game together."

He placed a six of diamonds beneath a seven of clubs. "I'm not asking *my parole officer* to hang out when she's doing a curfew check."

"So what? She's still human and she's nice, not to mention pretty."

Charlie glanced up from the cards, remaining silent. He wasn't about to agree. Not out loud anyway. But the thought of Mac made him feel warm all over. His body stirred just imagining how her long legs had looked in those tattered blue jean shorts. And the hesitant way she'd acted, embarrassed that he'd seen her in that outfit. Her modesty had been cute.

Hiding his thoughts, he shook his head at his sister-in-law.

"What? She is." Staring at the fire, Hannah propped her bare feet on the seat across the table. She wiggled her swollen feet out of her sandals. "I wish I had her hair. It's beautiful. Don't you think?"

The fire crackled in the silence as her question lingered in the darkness. Smirking, he finally said, "I don't think you'd look good with black hair."

She threw a potato chip at him. "That's not what I meant."

Footsteps echoed across the wraparound porch. Mac rounded the corner wearing athletic capris, an Aerosmith T-shirt, and gray Keds. Her hair was swept up in a messy bun, with loose strands cupping her slender chin. She slid a chair out from the patio table and slumped into it.

Glancing at Charlie, she gave him a faint smile, then looked at Hannah. Her gaze dropped to Hannah's belly. "You look so good. I can't believe you're in your third trimester."

"Thanks. I'm ready for this baby to pop out, that's for sure." Smiling, Hannah patted her stomach. "But I can't complain too much. Pregnancy definitely has its perks. The best part is your boobs get bigger."

It looked like Mac was about to smile, but then her lips drew into a thin line. The firelight flickered across her face, revealing tear-stained cheeks.

His chest constricted. Something was wrong with her. In all the times he'd seen her, she'd never looked so down. Hannah's suggestion resurfaced and against his better judgment, he decided she was right. "Do you have plans tonight?"

She eyed him curiously. "No. Why?"

"Want to stay and play cards with us?"

"It'd be much more fun with a third player." Hannah grabbed a handful of chips, popping one into her mouth.

"I, uh … I don't know. This was just a curfew check."

Charlie exchanged a glance with Hannah. *See, I told you so. I shouldn't have asked.*

Mac opened her mouth and shut it. "It's just … " She stopped midsentence, biting her bottom lip. "Is Daniel here?"

"He should be back in an hour or so." He furrowed his eyebrows. Why did she care if Daniel was home?

"He's down at The Joint drinking." Hannah rolled her eyes. "So what do you say? Will you play cards with us?"

"Well … " She looked distracted as she glanced at the house. "I guess I can stay for a bit."

"Perfect." Charlie grabbed the stack of cards and shuffled them. "Do you guys know how to play Slap Jack? Daniel and I used to play when we were kids."

Mac shook her head. "I've never played before."

Hannah smiled. "I'll teach you the rules."

Scooting back his chair, he stood and handed the deck to Hannah. While she explained the rules, he went inside the house to grab a few sodas. After setting the bottles on the table, he brought some logs back to the porch and opened the top of the fire pit, placing them inside. The fire sizzled back to life. He sat back down and took the deck from Hannah, shuffling the cards. "Ready to lose, ladies?"

Mac reached for a Coke, taking a sip. "A little too confident, are we?"

Leaning forward, he dealt the cards, his gaze resting on her. "I just want to prepare you. I'm the king of Slap Jack."

She rolled her eyes. "Highly doubtful."

Hannah laid an eight of spades. Mac set a ten of hearts on top. He put a jack above it. Mac slapped the pile first. He hit her hand, just a second too late for the win. It was a playful touch, but it sent electric tingles up and down his back. Too bad he couldn't keep his hand on hers longer.

Not seeming to notice his reaction, she grabbed the pile and held it in front of his face. "Ha. King of Slap Jack, huh?"

Shrugging, he held back a grin. "Beginner's luck."

"Oh yeah? We'll see about that. Go ahead."

He laid down a queen of diamonds. Hannah put an ace of spades above it. Mac set a two of clubs on top. He flipped over a jack. His hand shot out, smacking the top of hers.

Her soft laughter filled the night. "If you don't get faster, you might lose your position, your highness."

"Very funny." He smiled, liking the sound of her laugh. Whatever had her upset earlier, it didn't seem to bother her anymore. He hoped her mood had something to do with him, that he could make her feel better.

As the night wore on, darkness settled in and lightning bugs flickered through the sky. Hands turned red and the game remained competitive.

Mac slapped the pile again. "Yes!"

"Are you serious?" Hannah tossed her cards on the table. "I give up. You're on a roll."

Mac's grin widened. "I guess we all know who the losers are."

He shook his head. "Now who's being conceited?"

"Hey, I just call it how it is."

Smiling, Hannah gripped the arms of her chair, hoisting herself to a standing position. "I'm exhausted. I'm going to bed." Waddling to the door, she glanced back at Mac. "You should hang out with us again sometime."

The screen door swung shut, and Mac surprised him by staying seated. As she leaned back in her chair, a spectrum of conflicting emotions played across her face.

"A penny for your thoughts."

She made a steeple with her fingers. "I don't think you want to know."

"Try me."

"I was just thinking about Hannah and how uncomfortable she must be."

Charlie nodded. "She probably is, but she rarely complains about it. She's really excited to be a mom."

"Good for her."

"I get the sense you wouldn't feel the same way."

His comment seemed to take her by surprise. She shifted in her chair, fidgeting with a loose thread on her shirt. "I don't want kids."

His lips parted. "Why not?"

"What's the point of raising children in a world that's probably going to screw them up?"

"That's your reasoning?"

"Yeah."

"Why would you deprive yourself of having children just because you're scared of bad stuff happening to them?"

She stopped toying with the loose thread and met his gaze. "I'm sorry if I offended you, but it just doesn't seem worth it to me."

"You didn't offend me." He stared at her, mesmerized by the reflection of firelight in her eyes. "I think your reasoning is clouded, though. There's a lot of good in the world, too."

Her eyebrows furrowed together. "How can you say that after the way your life has turned out?"

Charlie jerked back. The bitterness in her tone hung in the air as they exchanged a long glance. His life definitely hadn't turned out like he'd imagined, but he wasn't going to roll over and play the victim.

Guilt flashed in her eyes. "I'm sorry. That was uncalled for."

He finished the rest of his soda and pointed the tip in her direction. "The better question is why *you're* letting someone or something stop you from having kids."

She diverted her gaze to the dwindling fire. "That's none of your business."

Heat crept up the back of his neck as he set the empty bottle on the porch. "Oh, so you can ask me all the personal questions, but I can't ask you any?"

She lifted her chin. "Yes, that's how this works. I'm your parole officer, so I get to ask the questions."

His gut soured at her reaction. He hadn't meant to offend her; he'd just wanted to point out her flawed reasoning.

She glanced down at her watch. "It's late. I better go." She stood up and headed toward the front of the house. "Whoa." Her arms flailed in the air as she tried to catch her balance.

He shot out of his chair and reached out, catching her in his arms. Her face was inches away from his as their eyes met and locked. A sweet, flowery aroma rose up from her neck. He drew in a breath, trying to slow his racing heart.

"Charlie, you can let go of me."

He swallowed hard, barely registering what she'd said.

"Charlie."

He spoke, his voice half-trapped in his throat. "Yeah?"

"You can let go of me," she repeated.

Reluctantly, he let go, and she slipped out of his grasp. He glanced down at the porch where his empty soda bottle lay near her foot. "Sorry."

She adjusted her shirt, pulling it down over her flat stomach.

He ran a hand through his hair and rocked back on his heels, then crossed his arms.

"I, uh … I'll see you next week." Mac spun around and walked away, her figure disappearing as she followed the wraparound porch out to the front of the house.

Charlie stood rooted in place. Her sweet fragrance still lingered behind. He closed his eyes, basking in the memory of holding her in his arms until reality settled in like an unwelcomed visitor. What was he getting himself into?

WIPING HER HANDS on her skirt, Mac peeked inside Warren's office. He sat hunched over his desk, a pen in one hand, a Sausage Egg McMuffin in the other. With a racing heart, she knocked on his door. "Can I talk to you?"

He looked up and smiled. "Of course."

She walked across his office and sat down in a chair in front of his desk. If he heard about her much too personal house check, he surely wouldn't have a smile on his face. He'd definitely think twice about recommending her for the Outstanding Correctional Worker award, if he was considering recommending her at all.

But mostly, he'd be disappointed in her unprofessional decision. At first, she'd wanted to stay, hoping Daniel would come home so she could observe his relationship with Charlie. But by the end of the card game, she'd wanted to stay to hang out with Charlie longer. If only their conversation about kids had gone better.

"What's up?" Warren asked.

She pressed her sweaty palms across her skirt as his steel-gray eyes bored into her, waiting for her to speak. The weight of her mistake sank into her chest as if he could see right through her. But he had no way of knowing that she'd hung out at Daniel's house last night, playing cards with Charlie and Hannah. He didn't know that Charlie had caught her in his arms, and despite what she'd said to Charlie, she hadn't wanted him to let go of her.

Warren leaned forward, his stomach pressing against his desk. "What's going on?"

Mac pushed loose hair away from her face. She had to forget about last night, at least for now. She had more important things to worry about. Like her dad lying unresponsive in a hospital bed, unable to wake up from his coma. Like her mom hiding liquor in the hospital room. Like whether or not Charlie should live with his patronizing brother.

Sitting up straighter, she crossed her legs and met Warren's gaze. "What can you tell me about Daniel Grimm?"

"Oh, well … " Pausing, Warren looked up at the ceiling as if the answers were written in the ceiling tiles. "I first met the Grimms when Veronica and Richard wanted to know about boot camps for delinquents. They wanted to send Daniel to a camp because he'd been getting into a lot of trouble."

"What kind of trouble?"

"When Daniel was a teenager, he tried to start a forest fire, he got into fights at school, and he vandalized the principal's house."

"You're kidding."

He shook his head. "I still can't believe it was Charlie who went to prison instead of Daniel."

"Then why did you ask Daniel if he'd let Charlie stay at his house? He doesn't seem like the most dependable person."

"After he went to the boot camp … " Warren took a bite of his sandwich, exposing a greasy, un-chewed piece of sausage as he spoke. "He was a different kid. Much better behaved."

She pursed her lips. "I'm still concerned. Daniel and Charlie aren't getting along."

"Are you sure Daniel's not just upset about Charlie turning down the position at Charger's?"

"That could be it. But I'm worried there's more to it, and I don't want anything to set Charlie back. From what I can tell, he's finally starting to adjust."

Smiling, Warren leaned back in his chair. "Sounds to me like you're warming up to him."

She shrugged. Better to have him think she was just warming up to Charlie, than to know just how attracted she was to him. "He has his moments."

"I knew you'd change your mind. It's hard not to like the kind of guy who would plead guilty."

She uncrossed her legs. "What are you talking about?"

Setting down his breakfast sandwich, he reached for a napkin and wiped his hands. "Charlie wanted to plead guilty immediately after his accident."

Her mouth went dry. "That's not in his records."

"That's because Veronica and Richard wouldn't let him. His parents wanted him to go to trial to fight for a lesser sentence." He dabbed the napkin on his lips. "Charlie was so distraught after the accident, I don't think he had much of a will to argue."

"Oh." Charlie's actions showed how willing he was to take responsibility for his actions. Not many offenders would do that, especially without knowing the charges first. A dull ache pulsated in her forehead. He was slowly becoming not only someone she liked, but someone she admired. If the roles were reversed, she wasn't sure she could've made the same decision.

An hour later, she stood on Daniel's front porch, knocking on the door. Her conversation with Warren had cast a whole new light on Charlie and she had to talk to him right away.

He answered the door shirtless with a towel draped around his neck. Dark brown hair sprinkled his tan chest and traveled down his sculpted abs, disappearing below his gym shorts.

Her mouth hung open and everything she'd planned on saying suddenly disappeared. Swallowing hard, she tried to regain her composure, forcing her gaze up to his face. "I, uh, I have something I need to talk to you about."

"Okay." He pulled the towel off of his neck and ran it through his wet, disheveled hair. A look of confusion crossed his face. "Do you want to come in?"

"No, I have to get back to work soon. I just have a quick question." She was completely downplaying the situation, but now that he was standing in front of her, his skin glistening like a Greek god, she had to at least pretend her emotions weren't running haywire.

He stepped out onto the front porch, closing the door behind him. "What's going on? You look like you just saw a ghost."

She tucked a strand of hair behind her ear. Obviously, she wasn't doing a very good job of pretending. "Why didn't you tell me you wanted to plead guilty?"

He rolled his towel into a ball, squeezing it between his large hands. "I didn't think it would matter."

She stepped closer to him, her gaze unwavering. "Why would you do that?"

"Because I deserved to go to prison." He said it matter-of-factly as if his reasoning was normal.

"Didn't you want to see what a judge would decide?"

"No."

"I don't understand you." She put her hands on her hips. "How can the same person who wanted to plead guilty also refuse to do a breathalyzer?"

He squeezed the towel so tightly drops of water dripped onto the porch. "I refused the breathalyzer after the police found the empty bottle of alcohol in my car. I knew it wouldn't change my charges, but I thought it would cause enough suspicion to get put away."

Her mind reeled. It really seemed like Charlie was telling the truth. But it still didn't add up. "Do you have any idea whose bottle it was?"

He shook his head.

"Okay, but I still don't get it. Why would you *willingly* go to prison?"

"I figured getting locked up was the only thing I could do to give Ally's family some sense of justice."

Her lips parted in awe. She had been so wrong about him. Not only did he feel immense guilt for his mistakes, but he'd also been willing to pay for them out of respect for Ally's family. *Holy crap. Charlie was the real deal—a genuine, good-hearted man.*

This really sucked. She'd finally met a man who met her standards, but she couldn't date him. A pinch of disappointment squeezed her chest. If only she had met him under different circumstances.

Chapter 10

"MORNIN.'" RAY WAVED at Charlie and set a warm plate of sprinkle-covered bones inside the glass display case.

Jackson dashed toward Ray, his tail wagging as he waited for a treat. Retrieving a bone, Ray cupped it in his palm and held it out to Jackson. The dog sniffed the treat before snatching it between his teeth, chewing just enough to swallow most of the bone.

Charlie hung his ball cap on the coatrack next to the door. The tension in his shoulders loosened. He would work all day to get a break from Daniel, who continued to belittle him for being a dog walker.

Ray gave Jackson another treat. "I never realized what an asset a dog would be around this store. I think people like seeing Jackson more than they do buying stuff for their own dogs."

"How come you never bring your dog with you?"

"Can you imagine a big greyhound in this little space?"

"No." Walking behind the counter, Charlie clocked in and glanced back at Ray. "Besides, people may like having a dog around, but you're the one they come to talk to. It's amazing how many customers you have already."

"You're just saying that because I'm your boss."

Charlie shook his head. "I'm saying that because it's true." He strode toward the door, turning the sign to Open. "You probably know more about your customers than most people know about their friends."

Ray bent down in front of the display case, adding fries and mini-burgers to the top shelf. "That's because I spent years as the high school football coach with everyone getting in *my* business."

The bells on the front door jingled. A woman wearing a sundress entered the store carrying a poodle in her arms. Shutting the display case window, Ray stood up and smiled. "Well, if it isn't Lyra. How's your fur ball doing?"

The woman sighed. "He's a little stinker. I'm still working on potty training and he's almost six months old."

Charlie stepped forward. "I can give you a few tips if you want."

Lyra's head turned in his direction, her cheeks turning crimson. She tucked a strand of hair behind her ear. "That would be great." She gave her poodle to Ray to start grooming and followed Charlie over to the counter.

He opened a book full of potty training tips. As he flipped through a few pages, Lyra leaned over the counter, exposing ample cleavage. She listened to him intently, and when he was done, he handed her a business card with the store's number. "Try those tips first and if they don't work, call me and I'll suggest others."

She glanced down at his left hand, and he grew increasingly aware that he no longer wore his wedding ring.

"Maybe we could discuss more tips over dinner sometime?" She wrote her number on the card and handed it back to him. Before he could respond, she walked toward the door, swaying her hips back and forth. With her hand on the door, she looked at Ray. "I'll be back in an hour."

Ray chuckled as hot air swirled across the floor and the door swooshed shut behind Lyra. He looked over at Charlie. "You know, she's single."

He smirked, redirecting the conversation. "See, I told you; you know everything about your customers."

"I thought you'd be interested in knowing, that's all. You're quite the catch. At least, the girls seem to think so."

"Okay."

Ray lifted the poodle onto the metal grooming table, removing the dog's diamond studded collar. "Haven't you noticed?"

He shrugged. "Yeah, but I'm not going to do anything about it."

"Why not?"

"I still love Ally." It was as simple as that. He didn't have room in his heart for another woman. And even if he did, he didn't deserve to find love again. It wouldn't be fair to Ally.

The old man slid a restraint over the poodle to keep him from moving. "That doesn't mean you should give up on dating, or marriage for that matter." Picking up a comb, he started brushing the dog's white curly hair. "Do you want to be alone for the rest of your life?"

Charlie reached for hair clippers and scissors, setting them on the counter close to Ray. He couldn't deny the loneliness that invaded his heart when he woke up and found the other side of his bed empty, or walked Jackson without holding someone's hand, or came home from work with no one to relax with on the couch. But none of it mattered.

"Did you forget that I went to prison? It's not going to be that easy," he mumbled.

"The right person will look past your background."

He wanted to tell the old man that he was wrong. No one would look past his background if he couldn't. And yet, he was fairly certain that Mac could and did. The way she looked at him the other day, like she was impressed with his attitude was proof enough, but she was his parole officer and completely off-limits.

Why did that fact bother him? Maybe it was the competitive part of him, wanting someone he couldn't have. That had to be it.

It made complete sense, but he knew he was lying to himself. He'd never met a woman quite like Mac. Her assertiveness, drive, and compassion kept him on his toes. And the more time he spent with her, the more his attraction grew. He wished he could run his hands through her long, dark hair or press his lips against hers or … He stopped his thoughts before they could go any further. No amount of wishing could change a thing.

MAC PARKED THE state car across the street from the Canine Palace. She slid out of the vehicle and drifted across the street, using all of her energy to fight off the exhaustion crawling through her brain.

How many hours had she slept last night—four, maybe five? Not long enough. But she couldn't sleep. Not after getting a call from Tucker, saying he'd arrested her mom for public intoxication.

If only her parents had listened to her, Jack wouldn't be in a coma and her mom wouldn't have been drunk at the hospital, yelling at the nurses.

She opened the door to the Canine Palace as two puppies stumbled out of the backroom.

Behind them, Charlie laughed and scooped the puppies into one arm, cradling them against his broad chest. He snapped a two-pronged leash to their tiny collars, then set the squirming puppies on the floor and rolled up a long sleeve shirt to his elbows, exposing tanned forearms with sun-kissed hair.

"Hey," she said, catching his attention.

Charlie smiled. "Ready?"

"For what?"

"We're going for a walk."

She glanced down at her high heels, frowning.

He followed her gaze. "You want to see what I do during my shifts, right?"

She nodded. "Let's make it a short one."

"You got it." Charlie reached for a ball cap stuffed into the large pocket of his cargo shorts and set it on his head. Thick brown tips curled out between the hat and his ears. He looked adorably boyish, and yet, as he led her to the bike trail, standing a full foot taller and smelling like musky cologne and a little sweat, she was reminded of how manly he was.

On one side of the path squirrels playfully scurried from tree to tree and on the other side, the nearby river swooshed against the shore. Above them, a blue jay glided across the path, singing a sweet melody. A light breeze fluttered across her face, and a pleasant chill ran up and down her body. This was much better than sitting in a stuffy hospital room, waiting to see if her dad would wake up. But maybe the chill had nothing to do with being outdoors and everything to do with Charlie.

For a while, they walked side by side. The path was narrow and more than once, his shoulder brushed against hers, and the sensation of his touch continued to linger. In the easy silence, her hands twitched at her sides, wanting to reach for his, but then her mind took over. *How stupid could she be?* Maybe this was how it had started out for her old coworker Gabe—innocent feelings that turned into more. But she wouldn't allow that to happen to her. She had more control of her emotions than that.

The puppies sniffed at a long-legged spider scurrying across the path. Barely escaping, the spider disappeared into the safe confines of grass.

Charlie shook his head at the puppies, gently tugging on their leashes. "Maddie, Kasi, let's go." They peered in his direction before taking off on the path again, walking in jagged, uncoordinated lines.

She chuckled. "I remember when Bruno was that young. His long ears would trail across the floor and he'd bump into everything. I couldn't even take him for a walk."

"I never used to walk Jackson much, before prison I

mean. I would've considered it a waste of time."

"Why?"

He strolled along the path in a comfortable gait and turned his head to look at her. "I was always busy."

"I know what you mean."

"It all seems so trivial now."

Nodding, she stood still as a boat sped through the water with a man jet-skiing behind it. Ripples spread across the glassy surface. Along the shore, lily pads bumped into one another playing a lazy game of bumper cars. The boat disappeared behind a bend in the river. The lily pads stilled, floating along the shore in serene tranquility. "I love being by the water."

He turned around and waited for her. "Good thing I took a job outside then, huh?"

"Too bad you're so difficult to put up with otherwise." She lengthened her stride to catch up.

Just as she stepped beside him, he moved forward, rushing ahead of her. "I'm difficult? Like when I patiently wait for you?"

She ran after him, grabbing for his arm. She caught him just above his elbow. His bicep bulged beneath her grasp as he stopped and turned, his face close to hers.

Her stomach dipped and spun in an airy summersault. His muscles were even harder than she'd imagined.

He glanced down at her hand, still circled around his arm, arching his eyebrow.

She let go, swallowing hard.

"Don't look so worried. You didn't hurt me."

"I know." She straightened her shirt and stepped into the grass, leaving a few feet between them. The distance made it easier for her to think. "How do you like the job so far?"

"It's been great. Ray's a little nosy, but I like the guy."

"Well, according to him, you're great with the customers and it seems like the dogs love you."

He nodded, a mischievous smile spreading across his face. "Keep going. What else am I doing right?"

"Fishing for compliments isn't a very flattering quality, you know."

He shrugged, his grin never fading. "Fine. I'll take what I can get. What else do you want to know?"

She pulled her hair up into a ponytail. That was all she needed to know. So they should turn around and head back down the trail, toward town. But this was her last meeting of the day. When it was over, she'd go back to the hospital. She quickly tried to think of something else work-related to lengthen their time together. "Did you get your driver's license yet?"

"Yeah, I did."

"Good. Have you changed your mind about driving?"

He shook his head. "No, I've told you how I feel

about that."

"Right." She looked out at the river again. The ripples had disappeared, leaving a flat, glossy surface. How different would her life be if it were calm like the water, especially when it came to her parents? They were a continuing wave of unsteady currents.

Charlie stepped closer, breaking the space between them and nudged her shoulder, definitely on purpose this time. "Are you okay?"

She stiffened. "Yeah." The less people knew about her personal life and her past, the easier she could maintain a strong persona needed for her job title.

As if sensing her hesitation, he stopped and looked directly at her, his unwavering gaze full of concern. "You should talk to someone about whatever you're going through. I didn't want to talk to you about Ally at first, but now that I have, I feel … " He looked at the sky as if the right words floated in the clouds. "Lighter. Like talking about her lifted a weight I never knew was there."

"That's great, but … " She couldn't finish the sentence; her throat was too dry. She shouldn't tell a client anything about her personal life. The way he was looking at her, though, made it seem like he actually wanted to hear what she had to say.

She took a deep, unsteady breath. "It's my dad. He's in the hospital."

"I'm sorry to hear that. Has he been sick long?"

"He's unconscious from alcohol poisoning."

Under the shadow of his hat, Charlie's eyes widened with sorrow. His concern tugged at her heart. "Did you know your dad had issues with alcohol?"

"Yeah. Both of my parents have been alcoholics and drug abusers since I can remember."

"It must have been tough growing up like that."

"It was." She should stop talking about her parents and end the explanation now, but the rusted floodgates had opened. Even though Jen and Tucker knew about her parents, she hadn't told them much about her childhood. Keeping her voice steady, she pictured night after night of her parents lying facedown between the soiled, crumpled sheets, the smell of alcohol infecting every inch of their apartment. "I never saw my parents doing drugs, but there were always people coming and going. I didn't think much of it, until I learned about drugs in school and realized my parents were selling weed."

"Wow. I never would've guessed you grew up that way. How did you turn out so well?"

His question made her feel oddly self-conscious. "I didn't want to be like them. They were so unhappy, always using alcohol to cope with their financial issues or their marriage problems. I hated living with them."

"I don't blame you. I would've been counting down the days until my eighteenth birthday, just so I could get out of there."

Heat crept beneath her cheeks. "Actually, I only lived with them until I was twelve."

"What happened?"

"It's a long story."

Charlie pointed at the trail stretching out before them. "We have plenty of time. I don't need to have these puppies back for another hour."

Her heels were biting into her feet, cutting into the skin around her ankles and toes. Tomorrow she'd regret walking any farther. She'd already told him too much, but the look in his eyes—part curiosity, part compassion—urged her on. "One night before my parents went out to the bars, I asked my mom for money. I really wanted to play soccer and I needed money for the uniform. When my dad wasn't looking, my mom took some of his booze money. I couldn't believe it. I was actually going to play."

She almost smiled, remembering the short-fused excitement of her twelve-year-old self. "The next morning, I was dressed and ready to leave for school when my parents came home, still wasted from the night before. I expected them to pass out right away, like they usually did. But my dad came into the kitchen and looked inside the cash bucket. He kept mumbling about paying someone back, so my mom told him she'd given the money to me."

Charlie frowned. "I don't like where this is headed."

"He started beating my mom. I thought he was going to kill her, so I went to the neighbors and called the police. When the police got there, they arrested my dad and took my mom to the hospital. Then they hugged me and told me that my parents were going away for a while." The officers had been her knights in shining armor, whisking her away from the angry, drunken man and the sad, scarred woman. "I was so relieved."

Charlie shook his head. "No kid deserves to grow up like that."

"My parents don't see it that way, not even now." They would never forgive her for calling the police, for sending them to jail and for taking away their drug business, their only financial stability.

"What happened after your parents went to jail?"

"I moved from foster home to foster home until I was eighteen. Not many people wanted me. I wasn't very nice to them." She looked out at the river as two teenagers kayaked close to the shore. "I just wanted adults to leave me alone, so I could take care of myself, like I'd already been doing for most of my life."

As they continued to walk, he watched her, and she couldn't deny liking the way it felt. "Is this why you work in law enforcement?"

"Yeah." She'd wanted to be just like her knights in shining armor, but unlike police officers, she didn't want to arrest criminals; she wanted to help them.

"No wonder you understand that a crime doesn't define a person."

She stopped walking. With most clients she understood this, all except Charlie. She'd been so wrong about him. And she couldn't look past her dad's mistakes either. How could she forgive him for the late drunken nights, her mother's bruises, and all his broken promises?

Charlie took her hand, his handsome brown eyes lingering on her face. "Do you feel better after talking about it?"

She couldn't look away, every muscle tensing at once. Her heart seemed to expand in her ribs, leaving little room for her lungs to breathe. The truth was, nothing could make the situation with her parents better, but right now she had a different issue. The way Charlie was looking at her made her heart pound uncontrollably in her chest.

She was in way, way over her head.

Chapter 11

CHARLIE SET A package of lunchmeat in his grocery cart. "Thanks, Gill."

"No problem." The grocer pulled off his latex gloves, making a snapping noise as they slid off of his hands. Peering over the deli counter, he pointed a finger at Charlie. "Don't be a stranger no more, ya hear?"

"You got it." Charlie turned his cart around to find more chocolate and pickles for Hannah. Someone had to fulfill her odd cravings and it certainly wasn't going to be Daniel. The farther along Hannah was in her pregnancy, the more Daniel worked, and the more help Hannah needed. Like someone to go to the grocery store so she could take a nap.

"Hey you," a female voice called from a few feet away.

Mac and Jen stood in front of the hamburger meat. Jen wore a pink sundress with dangling earrings, but his eyes locked on Mac, who wore a jean skirt and a white tank top. Her summer tan made her dark blue eyes stand out.

He resisted the urge to let his jaw drop. She looked good. Really, really good. His body stirred as he veered around a display of Styrofoam coolers, plaid tablecloths, and plastic silverware, and stopped his cart beside them. "You're a little dressed up for the grocery store, don't you think?"

"We're headed to the annual Victim's Rights Charity Picnic," Mac said.

He glanced down at their cart, almost filled to the rim with hot dogs, buns, ketchup, and mustard. "That's a lot of food for a picnic."

"Some of this is for the Cajun Food Festival on Saturday. We like to bring our own stuff. Some of that food is way too spicy." She grabbed another package of meat and tossed it in her cart. "Are you going?"

"Oh, I'm not sure." He'd been going to the festival since he was a little boy. Playing tag, running through the crowded streets with friends. Sampling shrimp Creole and jambalaya. Line dancing with Ally. Some of his favorite memories were at Maple Valley festivals, but going to the festival without Ally didn't seem right. "I don't think so."

"Why not?" Jen put a hand on her curvy waist, bracelets jingling. "Do you have other plans?"

"No."

Mac sent him a teasing grin. "You should go. I heard

that some up-and-coming rock band is playing."

"Why am I not surprised you want to go, then?" He returned her smile as a familiar bald man stopped beside them, carrying a bottle of margarita mix.

The blood drained out of Charlie's face. He would know this man anywhere. Officer Tucker, the police officer who had pried him off of Ally when the paramedics checked her vitals. The man who had held him back when the paramedics said the words he didn't want to hear.

Tossing the bottle in the cart, Tucker glanced at Mac. "I want to get some beer, too."

Mac sent Tucker a disapproving look. Did she think he'd judge her for drinking after knowing about her childhood? Hopefully, she knew that he wouldn't criticize her. If anything, he admired her for growing up in an abusive home and turning her life around. Not many people could do that.

Smiling at her for reassurance, Charlie nodded at Tucker, then looked back at Mac. "Have fun tonight."

He headed in the opposite direction, his mind reeling. Was this the same Tucker who Ray had referred to at the Canine Palace—the guy Mac had dinner with the other night? If so, the officer was probably her date to the picnic.

His chest tightened at the thought. Tucker wasn't just any officer. He'd witnessed the car accident. He'd seen Ally's lifeless body. No doubt the officer viewed him as a monster.

He rolled his head from side to side, trying to ease the tension in his neck. Had Tucker told Mac anything about the accident? If he had, Mac probably saw him as a monster, too.

Charlie sighed. Just when he was starting to feel human again.

DANIEL ROLLED OUT of bed and tiptoed to the closet. He slipped into jeans and a button-down shirt and snuck out the bedroom door. Hannah lay on her side in bed with an overstuffed body pillow between her legs. As he closed the door behind him, her incessant snoring sounded like a bull ready to charge. He rolled his eyes and crept through the dark hallway.

The floorboards creaked outside of Charlie's room. He stopped mid-step and listened for movement.

Thud.

His heart raced as the door inched open. He slunk against the wall. Jackson scrambled out of the room, growling.

He took a step backwards. "Shoo."

The hair on the back of Jackson's neck sprung up as he let out a bark.

"Bad boy," Daniel whispered. "Go away." He took off down the stairs with Jackson nipping at his feet. He kicked at the mongrel. Jackson whimpered and lowered his front legs, preparing to pounce.

He reached for his car keys and ran into the garage, slamming the door behind him. "That mutt better not wake anybody up." He hopped into his Ferrari and reversed out of the driveway.

The car hit something, followed by a shrill, clanking noise. He pushed on the brakes and rushed out of his car to see a trash can rolling down the driveway. "Could this night get any worse?" He bent down and checked his vehicle for scratch marks. Nothing. His shoulders relaxed.

He reversed onto the street, glancing at his house. The curtains in his bedroom slid into place. He stared at the darkened window, his back going rigid. No other movement surfaced. He scratched his head. Had Hannah seen him leave? He rubbed the sleep out of his eyes and continued driving. His mind was probably playing tricks on him.

Minutes later, a bright neon Open sign welcomed him inside The Joint. Willie Nelson's "You're Always on my Mind" floated from the jukebox. Two of his past teachers looked up from their game of pool, nodding hello. A gray-haired couple who knew his parents sat in a wooden booth, sharing an appetizer of onion rings.

"Hey, sugar." Standing behind the bar, Roxanne blew him a kiss.

He sat down on a stool, eyeing her up and down. Tonight she wore a leather skirt and a tube top that had dropped down to her cleavage. He slid his wedding ring off and hid it in the pocket of his jeans.

Roxanne sauntered over, swaying her hips. "What can I get for you?"

He forced his gaze away from her half-exposed breasts so he could look her in the eye. "Something strong."

She reached for a bottle of rum and poured the glass half full. "Tough week? You should have come in sooner." She leaned over the bar, her mouth close to his ear. "You know, I can make your week a whole lot better." Winking, she straightened and reached under the counter, mixing a small amount of soda with the rum.

Daniel shifted in his seat as his body responded to her. He knew what she was insinuating and that was exactly why he'd come here. But now that Roxanne was right in front of him, he wasn't so sure he could go through with it.

Roxanne set down a napkin and placed the dark, cloudy drink on top of it. "Made extra strong, just for you." She poured a shot for herself and held it high, winking at him again. "To tonight."

He twisted the shot glass in his hand. Could he sleep

with Roxanne? He loved Hannah, but the lack of intimacy between them lately had him on edge. He needed a release.

"Are you going to leave me hanging?" Roxanne protruded her bottom lip into a sexy pout.

He clinked his glass against hers. Just tonight, just this once, and he'd never cheat on Hannah again. Once she had the baby, she'd be back to her old self.

He chugged drink after drink and as the night wore on, a numbing dizziness draped over his brain. The older couple finished their onion rings and left. Following their game of pool, the teachers paid for one last round. Not long after, their motorcycles rumbled to life as they drove out of the parking lot.

Roxanne handed him another drink. She hiked her skirt a little higher. "I'm off in fifteen minutes. Do you want to go to my place?"

He could still back out. "I uh … " He reached out and touched her face. His thumb trailed down her cheek, landing on her lips.

She giggled.

His gut hardened. He couldn't do this to Hannah. Even if she never found out, she was the best thing that ever happened to him.

He dropped his hand. "I just remembered I have to be at work early tomorrow. I should go." His words ran together and he had to concentrate on each one.

Roxanne's face went blank as she stared behind him at the door.

Of course she was surprised. He'd been leading her on all night.

But the longer she stared at the door, the more he realized she wasn't reacting to what he'd said. He turned around on the stool, blinking to steady his vision. Blue and red lights flickered through the glass door. A bald police officer and a dark-haired woman barged inside.

"Roxanne Torrentino?" The police officer reached for a pair of shiny handcuffs attached to his belt.

"Yes," Roxanne stuttered. "That's me."

The officer hustled behind the bar and snapped the handcuffs on her wrists. Roxanne shook her head. "No, don't do this."

Daniel's gaze flickered from the officer to Roxanne. What was going on?

"Please, you don't understand. I couldn't find another job. I wasn't drinking, just working." Roxanne paused to look down at the police officer's name tag. "Please, officer … Officer Tucker." She stared at the woman next to the police officer. "Mac, you know how hard it is to get a job."

The dark-haired woman gave a sad smile. "I know it is, and you know the rules, Roxanne. You aren't supposed to enter a bar under any circumstances. You're also violating your parole curfew."

His eyes widened. Parole? What kind of woman had he almost slept with? He hazily stared at Roxanne, who suddenly went from an attractive, seductive woman to a slutty bartender.

Roxanne's lips trembled. "The money is for my kids."

Kids? She'd never said anything about kids. Daniel dropped his head in his hands.

"I'm sorry, Roxanne. After breaking these conditions, you can't get custody of them," said the dark-haired woman.

"I hate you!"

The woman turned to the police officer. "Get her out of here."

"You got it." The police officer jostled Roxanne toward the door. He looked at Daniel, then back at the woman. "Will you take him home? Judging by the looks of him, I highly doubt he can drive home safely."

Daniel narrowed his eyes. That cop wasn't talking about him, was he?

Roxanne and the officer disappeared and the dark-haired woman sat down on a stool. Her blue eyes seared into him. "You look familiar." She tapped a finger on her lips until recognition surfaced across her face. "You're Daniel Grimm."

He grunted. "What's it to you?"

"It's so nice to finally meet you, Daniel. How's your

wife?" Mac put her elbow on the counter, resting her chin on her hand. A derisive smile spread across her face.

He took a sip of his half-finished drink. Did he know her? She didn't look like someone he knew. She was pretty, though. Wait. Had she said his name condescendingly? His brain wasn't thinking quickly enough. "Who are you?"

"I'm a parole officer. Your brother's parole officer, in fact."

He choked on his drink, spitting some of it onto the bar.

She looked down at his ringless hand. "I must say you have some very nice wedding pictures hanging up around your house."

Daniel got off the stool and stood. The floor slanted beneath his feet. He clutched the counter to keep from spinning. "How dare you mock me! I've had enough of you."

She twisted on the stool, fully facing him. "Is that right?"

"You wasted my time. Charlie never wanted the job at Charger's."

"That was his decision, not mine." She glanced at the clock and slapped the bar counter. "It's late. I'm driving you home."

"I'll drive myself."

She slipped off the stool and stood next to him.

"You're too drunk to drive and if you get behind the wheel and start your car, I'll call the police. You wouldn't want a DUI, would you?"

Sneering, he stumbled toward the door.

"Before we leave, put your wedding ring back on," she snapped. "I happen to like your wife."

He shoved his wedding ring back on his finger and glared at her.

They exchanged a long look before she shook her head. "Your brother might have gone to prison, but he's a way better man than you'll ever be."

Daniel balled his fist and took a swing at her. Missing, he lost his balance and leaned forward, running into the door. Pain shot through his nose. Groaning, he cursed loudly and yanked the door open, stumbling out into the parking lot. He would get her back for this. No one humiliated him and got away with it.

He almost smiled. Poor parole officer, she had no idea what he was capable of.

CHARLIE TOOK OFF his seatbelt. "I can't believe you talked me into this."

Hannah parallel parked between a muddy Jeep Cherokee and a black truck with an *I'm an Iowa Corn child* sticker. She turned the ignition off and turned to

Charlie, giving him a coy smile. "I couldn't let you stay at home while everyone else is at the festival."

"Everyone, except Daniel." Charlie stepped out of the lime green Volkswagen and walked around to the driver's side, helping Hannah out of her seat and closing the door.

Frowning, Hannah adjusted her maternity dress across her belly and looped her arm around his. "Daniel has no idea we're gone. He's so hungover after last night he'll be sleeping all day."

Charlie snorted. "Yeah, that's true."

Crowds of people strolled down Ashmend Road with purple, green, and gold beads bouncing against their chests. Others gallivanted through the crowd wearing gold-feathered hats, purple boas, and green grass skirts. Little boys and girls ran between vendor trailers lining the sidewalks. Steam from the grills danced around the vendors' sweaty faces.

Seafood and bourbon saturated the humid air, mingling with excited voices from the crowd and light rock music from the band. A few people were already dancing in the street. He immediately felt the hole in his chest expand, wishing Ally were here.

But as he stepped off the curb, he scanned the busy street, his mind turning to Mac. She had to be around here somewhere. The curious part of him wanted to know if she was here with Officer Tucker.

Hannah pointed to a vendor with a striped purple and gold overhang. “Let’s sample the Cajun shrimp.”

“I have a better idea.” He lifted his chin, inhaling the spicy smells. His mouth watered. “Let’s sample everything.”

“I like your thinking.” She rubbed her hands together, excitement bubbling in her eyes. “Let’s do it.”

They walked from vendor to vendor, sampling the Cajun shrimp, crawfish, gumbo, chicken creole, and jambalaya. In between vendors, they stopped to talk to Ray Meyers, Gill, and a few of Charlie’s old friends. The conversations with his friends were awkward, just like he’d anticipated, but his buddies didn’t seem mad. If anything, the awkwardness seemed to come from the time spent apart, not because of the accident or prison.

The conversations didn’t last long, and as they strolled down the street, the sun lowered and the sky turned from baby blue to pink and orange. A light wind picked up, swirling through the sticky crowd. The stage lights turned on and the band encouraged people to start dancing as they mixed country hits along with their rock songs.

Charlie finished his last bite of chicken creole as the band started playing “I’ve Got Friends in Low Places.” He tapped his foot to the beat and sang along with the song, eyeing the crowd.

A few feet away, Mac stood on the sidewalk, sandwiched between Jen and the officer, her body turned in the direction of the officer. They were engrossed in a conversation. Watching them sent a pang right through him. He gripped the soda in his hand, and the plastic crackled beneath his grasp. Why, of all people, did Mac have feelings for Officer Tucker, the one person who had seen him at his worst?

Mac laughed at something the officer said, and he realized it was more than that. He liked being the guy who could make her laugh and it wouldn't matter what guy he saw her with, he'd probably still feel the same pang in his chest.

He squeezed the back of his neck. He had no right to be jealous. He was just her client, and when his parole was over, he'd just be a *former* client to her. His mind skidded to a halt as a new thought emerged. Or would he? Maybe once his parole was over, he would have a chance with her. Unless there were rules against that, too.

Just then, Mac glanced up from her conversation, meeting his gaze. Waving, she walked toward them, a grin stretching across her face. "I thought you weren't coming."

"I changed my mind."

"I'm glad." She bit her bottom lip. "I mean, for your sake. I think it's good to get out."

Silence settled between them as their eyes met, parted, and met again. She looked so cute in her denim dress that cut off just above her knees. Her dark hair was curled and draped over one shoulder. And her eyes—whoa—she'd put on more makeup than normal, a grayish-black highlighting her blue eyes.

He had to remind himself not to stare. *Not happening. Get your head straight.*

Hannah fidgeted with her purse strap, glancing between the two of them. "I need to go to the bathroom." She took his plate and threw it in a nearby trash can, then waddled off through the thickening crowd of dancers.

"What made you change your mind?" Mac asked.

"You and Hannah. The more I thought about it, I realized you were right. I need to stop hiding."

She gave him a teasing grin. "I'm right? You want to say that again?"

"You were right," he said, chuckling.

She smirked. "I'm glad you came to your senses."

His gaze flitted over her shoulder as the officer glared in their direction. Charlie grimaced, then tried to cover it up before Mac could see his expression, but it was too late.

"Is something wrong?"

He ran a hand over his mouth as he debated if he should tell her. "Did you know Officer Tucker was the one who arrested me?"

"Oh, uh … " She glanced over at the officer as Tucker rocked back on his heels with his thumbs hooked in the belt loops of his crisp pants. Meeting Charlie's gaze again, her cheeks reddened. "I knew." She said the words so quietly he almost didn't hear her.

"What did he tell you about my accident?"

She picked at the hem on her dress. Red blotches spread from her face down to her chest. "Nothing I didn't already know."

"You didn't ask him anything?"

"Why are you making such a big deal out of this?"

"I want to know, that's all."

Officer Tucker strode over and set his arm around Mac's shoulders. "Everything okay?"

She nodded, looking very comfortable beneath the guy's touch.

Charlie stared, a needle pricking at his heart. Was the officer her boyfriend? He wanted to ask, and yet, it wasn't any of his business.

Cutting off Charlie from view, the bald guy stood between them and pointed at people dancing on the street. "Want to dance, Mac?"

"Oh, um, sure." The last word came out rushed and sharp as she turned back to Charlie. "See you later."

He stood alone on the side of the street. The sun had disappeared below the horizon and now the moon cast a hazy glow on the festival. Cicadas buzzed from the nearby trees. Lightning bugs flitted through the warm spring air as children ran with their hands outstretched, trying to catch them.

Charlie kicked at an empty beer can. It rattled across the uneven brick. If Mac didn't know the gory details about his accident, then he'd pestered her for nothing.

He needed to apologize to her and he wasn't going to sit on the sidelines, waiting for his turn to talk to her.

He strode out onto the street, weaving between couples. He stopped beside Mac and the officer. "I wasn't done talking to her."

Tucker stopped moving and crossed his arms. The air changed, heavy and pressing. "How dare you—"

Mac held her outstretched arms between them. "Do you mind, Tucker? It'll just be a minute."

Sighing, the officer took a step back. "Come get me when you're done." He stalked off to Jen on the sidewalk.

With the bald guy gone, Charlie stepped closer to Mac. "I'm sorry for making a big deal out of nothing."

"Why does it matter if Tucker told me anything about your accident?"

He eyed the officer, who now stood beside Jen on the edge of the sidewalk, giving them curious looks. "Can we go somewhere more private?"

"Where?"

"Over there." He pointed to a deserted part of the street—a four-way stop where downtown met the residential neighborhoods. An orange and white Road Closed sign stood in the middle of the intersection, separating them from the festival.

Mac twisted her lips as if she couldn't decide if it was a good idea. After a moment, she shrugged. "Okay."

They stopped near the sign, and she lowered her gaze, digging the toe of her flip-flop into the pavement. "Why does it matter?" she asked again.

"I don't want you to know the guy I was that night."

She stopped moving her foot and looked up. "But I've read your files and you've told me what happened."

"I know, but I didn't go into all the details, like my arrest or what Ally's body looked like. Those are things I'm sure the officer remembers." He cracked his knuckles. "I'd rather you not know that stuff."

"That makes sense," she said quietly.

Now that he'd addressed *that* issue, he still wanted to know about her relationship with the bald guy. "I know it's none of my business, but are you dating that officer?"

She stared at him for a moment. "No. Why?"

He held back a smile, ignoring the sense of relief flooding through him. "Just wondering."

The band started playing "Just Another Day in Paradise" and increased the volume. Charlie held out his hand, palm up. "Dance with me?"

She stared at his hand as if it could bite her. "I'm not so sure that's a good idea."

"It's just a dance."

"I know, but … "

Charlie broke the distance and kept his hand held out. He understood her hesitancy, he knew the rules, but with the moon shining down on her, she looked like an angel. His heart skipped a beat, and he had a hard time thinking straight, making it difficult to find reasons not to enjoy the night together.

She slowly set her hand above his open palm.

Grinning, he pressed his other hand against her slender back, drawing her close. She hooked her fingers behind his neck, and he slid his arms tighter around her waist until there wasn't any space between them. They were so close he could feel the rise and fall of her chest. He lifted her arm above her head and gently pushed her back, propelling her to twirl.

Her arms relaxed as he reached for her hand again, swaying to the rhythm of the music. She looked up into his eyes. "Where did you learn to dance so well?"

"My mom made me take lessons."

"I'm embarrassed. You're much better than I am."

"You can't be good at everything. You had to take a cut somewhere, right?"

She laughed. "You're such a suck up. If I didn't know any better, I'd think you were buttering me up. Trying to make sure I discharge you from parole, so you can get rid of me."

"On the contrary, Miss Christensen. I enjoy spending time with you." He tightened his grip on her back, dipping her as their gazes locked. "Honestly, spending time with you is the best part of my week."

With her back curled above his arm, she stopped moving and a smile spread across her face. "Is that so?"

He nodded and brought her back to a standing position. The moon cast a light on her face as she peered up at him, her lips parting. For a moment, it was easy to forget how their paths had crossed—until he glanced over her shoulder.

Officer Tucker and Jen stood by the Road Closed sign, their eyes filled with disapproval.

Chapter 12

MAC STRETCHED OUT her legs on the reclining couch and pulled Bruno onto her lap. Picking up the remote, she turned on the TV. Background noise would help drown out her busy mind. Her dad was still in the hospital unconscious. If he didn't wake up soon, her mom would have to make a decision—keep him on life support or take him off of it.

Lynn might have difficulty deciding what the right choice was, but if *she* had a say in the matter, it wouldn't be hard. He'd abused her mom for too many years. And the longer Jack stayed unconscious, the easier it was to see he wasn't coming back. If only her mom would stay sober long enough to give consent.

The door to her condo swung open and shut. Jen walked into the living room dressed in a casual summer dress. She'd gone out with Tucker's new partner from the police department almost every night this week.

"Did you have fun with Scott?"

Her roommate plopped down on the couch, her eyes

lit with excitement. "Yeah, I really like him. He took me to Candy Galore and we shared an ice cream sundae."

"Yum, that sounds good."

Jen pulled her legs onto the couch, sitting cross-legged. "Did you go to the hospital tonight?"

"Yeah."

"How's your dad?"

"He still isn't showing any sign of brain movement. The doctor isn't sure he'll wake up."

Jen patted Mac's leg. "I'm so sorry."

"I think the not-knowing part is the hardest, you know? Will he wake up or won't he?"

Jen nodded, seemingly at a loss for what else to say. Mac didn't blame her. She'd never talked much about her parents before this happened, so her roommate wasn't quite sure how to comfort her.

She surfed through the channels, searching for one of Jen's favorite reality TV shows. Her finger paused above the button when a familiar set of actors appeared on the screen. A woman yelled at her boyfriend, her arms swinging in all directions.

Jen leaned over and turned up the volume on the remote. "I love this part. She just caught her boyfriend cheating."

"I wish Hannah would do the same," Mac mumbled.

"Who's Hannah?"

"Oh, I forgot to tell you about Charlie's brother."

She turned to Jen, adjusting Bruno on her lap and explained what had happened at The Joint.

Jen's eyes widened. "No way."

"Yeah. And Daniel wasn't wearing his wedding ring. So I'm pretty sure he was planning to cheat on his wife."

"That's horrible. Are you going to tell Charlie?"

"I would want to know if I were Hannah, but it's not like I caught him in the act. He hadn't done anything wrong yet."

Jen scoffed. "Maybe not that night, but he's probably been doing it for a while."

"Probably. I feel so bad for Hannah, and Daniel's not nice to Charlie either." She sat up straighter and leaned forward, resting her elbows on her knees. "I wish I knew why."

Jen slid off the couch and opened the screen door, letting in the warm summer air. Voices rose from the street below as people left Val's Diner. "I think you have more important things to figure out."

She glanced down at her hands, afraid of what her roommate was implying. "What are you talking about?"

"Your feelings for Charlie." Jen walked into the kitchen and opened the fridge, hunching over to search through the contents. "I saw the way you looked at him at the festival."

Heat rose to her cheeks as Jen's red mane popped up above the fridge door. "You need to be careful." Her roommate poured a glass of lemonade and shut the fridge, returning to the living room. “Sure, Charlie’s hot, but come on. There are a lot of other guys out there who you’ve never given the time of day to, and *they* can’t interfere with your job.”

“He’s just a client. That’s it.” If only it was true, but lately, she couldn’t deny her feelings for Charlie were growing stronger. Dancing with him at the festival had felt so right. It was hard to believe they’d only known each other for a couple of months. It felt much longer than that. He was someone she could open up to. The way he listened made her feel like the only person in the world. And even though he was a dog walker now, he was still looking for other jobs, determined to maintain a career. Plus, the way he cared for Hannah was so sweet. No doubt he’d make a good husband one day.

The longer she let her thoughts go on, the guiltier she felt. What the heck was wrong with her, thinking about Charlie as a husband?

Jen gave her a knowing look as if she could see right through her. “He might be a great guy, but nothing will ever change the fact that he’s an offender.”

“I know.”

“I can’t believe you would risk it, especially after Gabe got fired.” Jen sat back down on the couch next to her.

She glanced at Bruno, playing with one of his ears. “I

won't do anything stupid."

"Good. I'd hate to see you lose your job because of a relationship with a client."

"I'd never let that happen." She couldn't risk her career for him. She loved being a parole officer. It was the perfect job for her. She enjoyed helping people change their lives for the better. But since meeting Charlie, her world had turned upside down. He'd encouraged her to open up and have fun—things she never allowed herself to do. She wasn't thinking straight. That was the problem. In fact, she wasn't thinking at all.

Rules were rules and there was no use questioning them.

"WE NEED TO talk." Mac aired out her dress shirt, pulling it away from her warm skin. She really needed to tell Charlie that they were overstepping boundaries: hanging out, playing cards, dancing at the festival. People were starting to notice. Jen had made that quite clear. This relationship would never go any further than a parole officer and a parolee.

"What's up?" Charlie stopped along the trail, waiting for Jackson and a collie. They inched down the trail with their tongues hanging out. The collie ambled into the grass and lifted her leg, peeing on a tree. As he waited for the dog, he glanced at Mac.

"We can't—" A rumble of thunder reverberated overhead. Menacing clouds moved swiftly across the sky. She frowned. It looked like it would pour down at any minute. "I think your brother might be cheating on Hannah. I saw him at the bar without his wedding ring on." Not exactly what she'd intended on saying, but Charlie needed to know about Daniel too. For Hannah's sake.

Charlie's lips parted. "Are you sure?"

"I'm not one hundred percent positive, but I can tell you what I saw. I went to The Joint to arrest a client, and I saw your brother leaning over the counter, touching the bartender's lips with his fingers."

His jaw tightened. "How could Daniel do that to Hannah?"

"Maybe you could ask him about it. Hopefully, I'm wrong."

Charlie shook his head. "You make it sound so simple. Daniel will think I'm accusing him."

"If he is cheating, you can't let him get away with it. Think of Hannah."

"I'll come up with something to get to the bottom of it." He growled. "Let's drop it for now. I hate talking about my brother."

Mac nodded as thunder boomed in the sky. She stopped midstride. "We should head back."

He waved his hand with indifference. "Don't be such a girl. This weather is perfect." He sent her a sideways grin, giving her stomach butterflies.

"Are you acting sexist on purpose, just to make me mad?" She narrowed her eyes.

Charlie laughed. The collie crossed back onto the trail and he caught up to where she was waiting. "I like getting a rise out of you. You get all defensive before you realize that I'm joking. It's cute."

She put her hands on her hips. She should be upset by his comment, but she couldn't help feeling pleased. "Oh, I'm supposed to feel better then? You're sadly mistaken. I could write you up for that, you know."

"Fine. I dare you."

"Are you in second grade?"

He nudged her in the ribs. "Maybe … "

She shook her head and took a step away from him as Jen's warning returned all too quickly. After all that talk about Daniel, she still hadn't addressed their much too close relationship.

Thunder roared again and rain splattered across the pavement like soup boiling over onto a stovetop. She wiped drops off her cheek. "I told you we should've turned back."

The clouds turned from gray to charcoal black. Lightning flashed across the sky. She took brisk strides back down the path, not willing to wait for him.

"Hold on," he said.

She turned around to face him. He stood still with a childish grin spread across his face as rain poured down from the sky. They were both soaked. Using her free hand, she tugged at her clinging shirt, ready to bolt. "What are we waiting for?"

He took the collie's leash and tied it around an oak tree. Stepping back on the trail, he tilted his head back and closed his eyes. Rain splattered across his face. His hair fell flat across his forehead. "I want to enjoy this."

She crossed her arms as he twirled around on the pavement with his arms outstretched. "You're crazy!" she shouted above the rattling thunder.

He stopped and teetered off the path before regaining his balance. "Come on, try it." He reached for her hand and pulled her closer.

She bit her lip. She should say something now. To stop this, whatever *this* was. But Charlie stared at her expectantly and she couldn't tell him to stop. This was the most carefree he'd ever been and she didn't want to take this moment away from him. She squeezed his hand. "Why not?"

He moved his shoes in front of hers and leaned back, tilting his head toward the sky. His hands gripped hers as they twirled together.

The world spun around her, blurring green and brown images into a colorful fusion. Laughter bubbled in her chest as she looked at Charlie with his boyish face and cheesy smile. Giggling harder, she stumbled backward. He caught her, gently pulling her upright until their faces were inches apart.

Swallowing hard, she forced her head to turn away from him, breaking the spell. She let go of his hands and took a step back.

Lightning lit the dark sky as hail dropped from the looming clouds, pounding on her head and her shoulders. She took off down the path and covered her head with her hands.

Charlie caught up to her with the dogs running beside him. "We're not too far away from Candy Galore; it's the closest store to the trail. Let's go in there!"

She nodded and sprinted down the rest of the way. In front of Candy Galore, she thrust the door open and dashed inside.

A puddle of water formed beneath her wet flats. Charlie pulled the door shut behind them and stripped off his shirt, twisting it.

Her gaze traveled up and down his muscled arms, well-built pecs, and chiseled abs. Her stomach flipped and filled with warmth.

He caught her staring at him, and she looked away, glancing around the store. *Focus, Mac… Focus on anything except him.* The empty shop was designed like a 1950s ice cream parlor. Red cushions covered the booths.

The floor was checkered with black and white squares, and Betty Boop and Coca-Cola signs decorated the pink walls.

"It looks like we're stuck here until the hail lets up." He put his T-shirt back on and ran a hand through his wet hair. Drops washed across his forehead and dribbled down to his square jaw. She had the sudden urge to lift her hand and wipe the drops away from his face.

Instead, she crossed her arms and looked directly in his eyes—the safest place on his body that wouldn't lead her thoughts astray. "I can't stay here. I don't have time." She had a meeting in an hour and had client files to attend to, which she'd wanted to finish by this afternoon.

"I don't think you're going anywhere soon."

She glanced out the window. Rain and hail still fell from the dark sky. If she left now, she'd get pelted with hail. Her car was over a block away.

A white-haired woman came out from the back room, wearing a petticoat and a shiny pink jacket. "Caught in the brewing storm, were ya?" She caught sight of Charlie, a wide smile spreading across her face, exposing yellow, crooked teeth. "It's about time you visited me. I've missed you, darlin'."

"It's good to see you, Sandy." He approached the woman and bent down to hug her. "How've you been?"

"I'm old. How in tarnation do you think I've been?"

He chuckled. "Do you mind if we stay here until the

downpour stops? I promise the dogs won't make a mess."

"You know you're welcome here anytime. Let me get you some towels." She turned around and disappeared behind a creaking door. A minute later, she returned and handed them a couple of towels.

Mac slipped the ponytail band out of her hair and shook the towel through her loose strands. She wiped off her dress pants and shirt as best as she could. As she did, Charlie eyed her up and down, and she resisted the urge to smile. *Had he really just checked her out?*

Clearing his throat, he looked away from her and walked to a booth by the window. He slid into the seat, and scooted over as Jackson jumped up beside him and the collie lay down beneath the table. He grabbed two menus and held one out to her. "Let's get some ice cream while we wait."

She slid into a seat across from him. This was so, so wrong, but what else could she do? She couldn't go outside with the hail. Surely, Warren would understand if he asked her about it. Since she was stuck, she might as well enjoy the break from work.

She took the menu and scanned the list of malts, sundaes, and candies. Her nose wrinkled in disgust. "Chocolate-covered gummy worms? I love gummy worms, but I'm not a fan of chocolate."

He winked. "I thought every woman liked chocolate."

"I'm not going to say anything to that. If you don't get a rise out of me maybe you'll stop."

"Nah, I won't stop. You like it too much."

Sandy sashayed over to the table in her pink skirt, her gaze locked on Charlie. "I assume you want to order the usual."

Mac eyed Charlie, her chest tightening. He'd probably come here with Ally many times. She cleared her throat, trying to swallow the sudden twinge of jealousy. "What would you suggest, Sandy?"

"Root beer floats are my favorite."

"I want a root beer float then," Mac said.

"I'll have the same." Charlie closed his menu with resolve.

"Be back in a jiffy."

As Sandy walked to the kitchen, Mac shook her head at Charlie. "You're such a copycat."

He set the menus back in the metal holder. "Now who's in second grade?"

"Apparently, we both are." She leaned back against the booth. "I can't help it. I feel like a kid. I've never been in a candy store before."

"Really? You don't get out much around here do you?"

"No, and I should. This downtown area is one of the reasons I moved here. I like how historic it looks."

"Most of the shops in Maple Valley were built in

the '60s." Charlie opened his arms wide and rested them on the back of the booth. "If you can't tell, not much has changed around here."

"I like it that way. There's a lot you can learn about history in an old town."

"Have you ever noticed that you can learn a lot wherever you are?"

"You're probably right." She unfolded the napkin around her silverware. "Are you referring to prison?"

"No, I was thinking about your office."

"My office?"

"Yeah, it's really plain." He leaned forward, setting his elbows on the table. "But the longer I've gotten to know you, I've realized it's just because you're a guarded person."

She stiffened. "It's required to be that way. If I had anything personal in my office, it would give clients too much information about me."

"Oh, I guess that makes sense."

"But you're right about one thing. I am a guarded person."

"I'm glad you've opened up to me." He reached for the chocolate syrup and slid the container across the table between his hands. "But there is one thing I'd still like to know."

She gave a nervous laugh. "What is it?"

"I noticed the tattoo on your back when we were at

the dog park. What does it symbolize?"

"It's a koi fish. In the Japanese culture, koi symbolize overcoming adversity." She unfolded her silverware, setting a napkin in her lap. "There are stories about koi climbing up waterfalls. They say it's possible because the fish are so determined to reach the top of the waterfall that they persevere and succeed."

"Wow, that's really cool."

"Here we go." Sandy brought the root beer floats in tall frosted mugs. When she walked away, they ate in silence.

Mac stirred melting ice cream with fizzing root beer, ignoring her racing heart. She felt giddy, like a high school girl on her first date. She hadn't felt this way in a long time.

Charlie cleared his throat and dipped his spoon in the ice cream. "Hannah started painting the baby's room."

"Are you excited to be an uncle?"

"Yeah, but I probably won't see the baby much. As soon as my parole is over, I'm moving."

Her head jerked up. "Why?"

"I want to start over somewhere else, someplace no one knows me."

She stopped stirring her dessert, her stomach sinking. If he moved, she'd probably never see him again. Sudden remorse nudged her to persuade him to stay. "It sounds like you're just running away."

He shrugged. "There's nothing wrong with wanting a fresh start."

"That's true, but you've already started over here. You have your job at the Canine Palace. And too many people would miss you." Including her, not that she would tell him that.

Sandy neared the table and set the bill down. She pointed a long, yellow thumbnail at Charlie. "She's right. We just got you back. You can't leave already."

He glanced up at the shop owner. "Why not?"

"I need a strong young man like you to fix things around my house. My back is starting to hunch. Pretty soon I'm going to look like the hunchback of Notre Dame."

He gave her a kind smile. "You still look beautiful to me."

"You sure know how to win a woman's heart, Charlie Grimm." Her cheeks flushed as she placed a wrinkled hand over her heart.

Mac's stomach churned. Sandy was right. Charlie was awfully charming when he wanted to be. At the festival, she'd joked with him about sucking up to her, but maybe he *was* purposely flattering her just to get discharged from parole sooner.

Could it be true? If Charlie was playing her, she was just as blind as her mom when it came to men. The thought left a bitter aftertaste in her mouth.

Chapter 13

A KNOCK RAPPED on Mac's office door. Warren's voice carried from the other side. "It's me."

Her heart picked up speed. He must have heard about her and Charlie at Candy Galore. Would that be enough to start an investigation? Was her job on the line?

Two loud knocks banged on the door again.

"Just a sec." She moved around her desk and walked across her office, unlocking the door with shaky hands.

Warren stood with his arms crossed above his stomach, blocking the entire doorway. "I have something I'd like to discuss with you."

Her stomach dropped like she'd just gone down the big hill on a roller coaster. "Come on in." She tried hard to keep her voice steady. "I was just working on some client files."

"Ah." Shuffling his feet, he plopped into the chair across from her desk. The leather chair sank beneath his weight with a soft swoosh. "This will just take a second." He gave her a curious look. "Are you going to sit down?"

Her face flushed as she shut the door and sat down behind her desk.

Warren leaned forward in his chair and handed her a paper. "Why haven't you registered for the ICA Conference?"

She held the paper between her fingers and read the contents, expelling a relieved breath. He hadn't heard about Candy Galore. Her job wasn't in question. But now she had a different problem: the Iowa Corrections Association conference was scheduled in two weeks, and she'd completely forgotten about it.

Without waiting for her answer, Warren continued. "I didn't want to tell you, but you leave me no choice. I recommended you for the Outstanding Correctional Worker award. You need to go to the conference, in case you win."

She dropped the paper, letting it drift onto her desk as she put a hand over her chest. "Oh, Warren. I'm so honored. Thank you."

"No need to thank me. You deserve it. You're one of the best parole officers in this building. You're gonna go far, kiddo."

A mix of emotions swirled through her—delight, nervousness, and guilt. Of all the other parole or probation officers Warren could've nominated, he'd chosen her. She could win one of the most prestigious awards of her career. And yet, did she deserve it? Sure, she'd made a difference by recreating offender programs and earning grants, but she had feelings for Charlie. She'd broken the one rule that could jeopardize her job and a client's progress.

Heat crept up the back of her neck. She slunk back against her chair, pasting a smile on her face. "I'll register for the conference right away."

"Great." Warren heaved himself up. Walking to the door, he turned around, smiling mischievously. "Oh, and ask Officer Tucker to come with you. I heard he's a good friend of yours."

She sighed. Why did everyone want her to date Tucker? They must see something she couldn't see. Maybe she did have potential with Tucker. She'd refrained from dating colleagues for so long, it was hard to tell. Maybe asking Tucker to go to the conference was exactly what she needed to get her mind off of Charlie. And it would surely get Jen off her back and anyone else who was starting to notice her feelings for him.

CHARLIE SHUFFLED A deck of cards and arranged them for another game of solitaire. He needed something to keep his mind off of his last meeting with Mac—if you could even call it a meeting. It sure hadn't felt like it; it had felt like a real date. And for the first time since he'd been released from prison, going on a date felt good, as if moving on might be okay after all.

Spending time with Mac at Candy Galore had almost made him forget about Daniel. But that was still at the back of his mind too. Bile rose in his throat. How could Daniel cheat on Hannah, especially when she was pregnant? He didn't want to start an argument with Daniel, but he couldn't let his brother get away with it. Somehow, he'd find out the truth.

Out in the yard, Jackson barked at two squirrels running across the yard. He dashed after them, toward the woods, his tail wagging back and forth.

"Jackson, stay in the yard." With the porch light extending over half the yard, visible safety only reached so far. The black shadows could swallow any living creature prowling through its depths, especially a small, housebroken dog.

The back door opened. "Mind if I join you?"

Charlie jumped, and the two of hearts fluttered to the porch.

"Did I scare you?" Hannah asked.

He scowled, pretending to be offended. "I don't get scared."

"Uh-huh, sure." She stepped onto the porch wearing yoga pants and a loose T-shirt. She plopped into a folding chair, her legs jerking up like a doctor had whacked her knees. She blushed and rubbed her growing stomach. "Ah, that feels better."

He leaned down and picked up the two of hearts. "Want to play a card game?"

"Not tonight." She pulled her short hair into a small, messy bun. With the hair away from her face, her cheeks appeared plumper and the bags under her eyes were more noticeable.

No wonder she looked exhausted. He'd woken up to the sound of her toilet flushing at least four times last night.

"Charlie?" As soon as she had his attention, she looked down at the glass of water held between her hands. She wiped off the dripping condensation with her thumb. "I have a question to ask you, and please feel free to say no if you want."

"Anything."

"Would you help me finish painting the baby's room?"

"Sure, but doesn't Daniel want to do it?"

She shook her head. Loose strands escaped beneath the hair tie and framed her round face. "He's too busy with work. And it's taking me forever. I shouldn't be around paint fumes for too long."

"No problem. I'll do it."

"Thank you." She looked at him through tear-filled eyes. "Sorry, I guess I'm a little emotional these days."

Charlie forced himself to smile. He could only hope

work was the reason Daniel was so busy. Either way, Daniel had no idea what he missed when he made anything else a priority over his family. Everything could be gone in an instant. Charlie knew that all too well.

Hannah wiped a tear from her cheek. "It's nice having someone around at night. Daniel is gone so much."

He gave her a reassuring smile. "My job definitely has its perks."

"I'm glad that everything worked out for you. I can tell how much you enjoy your job. It's crazy to think you were going to be the owner of Charger's."

He stopped playing. "I *think* my dad would've promoted me, but I don't know that for sure."

Hannah covered her mouth. "I shouldn't have said anything."

"What do you mean?"

"Please, forget I said anything."

He tossed the cards on the table, staring at her. "Hannah, what are you talking about?"

She pressed her lips together and looked out at the yard. "I thought you knew."

"Knew what?"

She lowered her chin and heaved a sigh. "Your dad told Daniel that you were going to be the owner when he retired. Your parents wanted him to know before they promoted you because they knew he'd be disappointed."

His mouth fell open. Years ago, he'd hoped to receive

the promotion over Daniel, but then the car accident happened. In prison, he'd never asked his dad about Daniel's promotion, choosing to take comfort in the unknown.

"I shouldn't have said anything. Don't be mad."

Charger's Sporting Goods could've been his. Nine years of long hours and coming home to a frustrated wife begging him to cut back his time at work. It hadn't been for nothing. His dad had believed in him. "If you had worked all your life to get something and then you lost it in the blink of an eye, wouldn't you want to know that you'd still earned it?"

"Yeah." Hannah's lips trembled. "But like I said before, at least everything has worked out with your job."

"It's not going to pay the bills. I'll have to find something else in a few months. I can't live on minimum wage for the rest of my life."

"I'll help you in whatever way I can."

Charlie turned to her with a resigned frown. Why would Daniel keep this from him? His brother definitely had some explaining to do.

MAC OPENED THE door to room 340. Her dad lay motionless on the hospital bed. Tubes snaked through his nose and slithered across the floor attached to a machine that gave a steady *beep, beep, beep*.

Walking across the room, she sank into a chair next to the bed and clasped her hands above her legs. She looked down at Jack. Thin strands of black hair lay matted against his pale, wrinkled forehead. Dark shadows creased the skin beneath his closed eyes.

She was close enough to touch him, and she supposed most daughters would reach out to hold their dad's hands. But she detested the hands that had slapped, shaken, and cut Lynn. Those hands had done too many evil things.

The hospital door opened slowly. Her mom shuffled into the room. "What are you doing here so early?"

Mac shrugged. "Couldn't sleep."

Lynn sat down on the bed next to Jack and ran her hand across the stark white blanket. "I should have propped up his head with pillows. Maybe he wouldn't have started choking that day."

"This wasn't your fault. He's the one who got drunk and passed out."

Lynn studied Jack before lifting a hand to smooth his hair. "How can you say that with your dad in a coma?"

"Stop defending him."

Lynn didn't look away from Jack, her lips forming a thin line. "Then stop acting like you're some wounded kid. You turned out all right."

She flinched. Her mom didn't get it. She'd rewritten

history in her mind, as if Mac hadn't grown up seeing the terrors of Jack's alcohol abuse. "If he wakes up, he's not going to change." Even if her mom remembered the past differently, maybe she'd listen now that Jack was unconscious. "This is the perfect time for you to leave him."

The quiet whisper of the ventilator filled the room before Lynn looked up at Mac wearily. "Aren't you tired of this conversation? I sure am."

"Please," she said in a quiet tone.

Lynn pulled the blanket higher on Jack, covering his shoulders. "We don't know how much longer he has. You should be saying good-bye if … " She couldn't finish the sentence as tears streaked down her cheeks.

Mac leaned forward, resting her elbows on her knees. "I'll take you apartment hunting. I'll help you find a job. This is what I do for a living. Let me help you."

Her mom snorted. "I don't need help from *you*."

A long, shrill noise came from the heart monitor.

Mac remained frozen in her chair. Lynn jumped up from the bed and pressed the button for help. Nurses raced into the room. One grabbed a defibrillator and pressed it against Jack's chest. His body jumped from the bed before collapsing back onto it. Another nurse leaned close to his face and started mouth-to-mouth resuscitation.

"Save him." Lynn covered her mouth with her hands.

Mac stood, her whole body trembling. Jack was dying right before her eyes. How many times as a child had she wished for this to happen? If only to save her mom.

"Hold on, baby. Don't die," Lynn pleaded.

The nurses tried the defibrillator again. The machine's shrill scream continued to pierce the room as a straight line scrolled across the screen. The doctor rushed in and checked for a pulse. She glanced at Mac, then Lynn, a solemn look spreading across her face. "I'm sorry. He's gone."

"No, no, no." Lynn collapsed on the floor, sobbing. "What am I going to do?"

Mac looked at Jack, now lying completely motionless on the bed, and expelled a breath. He could no longer hurt her mom. She bent down next to Lynn and rubbed her back. "I'm so sorry."

Mascara ran down her mom's cheeks as she pushed her hand away. "No, you're not. You're not even sad. This is all your fault."

The blood ran out of her face. "What?"

"You upset your father. He probably heard all those things you said about me leaving him." Lynn wrapped her frail arms around her body and rocked back and forth on her knees. "I hate you."

The words sliced through the room like a machete, cutting away at the small piece of hope she'd been holding on to. Her mom could have turned to her. They could have comforted each other. But it was clear now: Lynn only wanted her husband. And he was gone.

Lynn glared at her, blue eyes as cold as ice. "I never want to see you again. Do you understand me? Leave. Me. Alone."

With her heart aching, she stood and stumbled out the door. In the hallway, she collapsed against the wall. Her mom's words would always haunt her. *I hate you. I never want to see you again.*

She buried her head in her hands, lowering her chin to her chest. She'd failed. Her mom would never change. Nothing she said or did would ever make a difference.

Why had she even bothered trying to help? She'd never meant anything to her mom. And now she never would. She wouldn't try anymore; she couldn't. She had nothing left to give.

MAC WOKE UP, blinking several times. Bright fluorescent lights illuminated the hospital hallway. Wiping her eyes, she stretched her aching back, glancing up at the clock in the hallway. 7:30 a.m. No way would she make it to work by eight. She pulled her cell phone out of her pocket and left a voicemail on Warren's machine, telling him she needed the day off. She couldn't face anyone from work in this emotional state.

After making a trip to the bathroom, she wandered down the hospital hallway and drifted down the stairs, stopping on the second floor. She couldn't leave the hospital, not yet. If she went back to her condo, Jen would be at work all day, and she would be completely alone.

She opened the door on the second floor.

A woman dressed in blue scrubs stood up behind a half-circle counter. "Who are you here to see?"

"I'm sorry. I'm not here to ... " She stopped speaking as a nurse walked past her, pushing a woman in a wheelchair. The woman clutched a baby wrapped in a pink blanket. Mac smiled at the woman, and just as she was about to turn around, she noticed a man who looked a lot like Charlie. He was standing in front of a large glass window, dressed in sweatpants and a Canine Palace T-shirt.

She did a double take, her eyes widening. It was Charlie. She looked at the woman behind the counter for approval. "I'm here to see the Grimm family."

"Okay, go ahead."

She gave the nurse a weary nod and ambled toward Charlie.

As she drew near, he noticed her. Disheveled hair lay matted across his head and sleep lines ran across his cheek. "Mac?" A big grin spread across his face. "How did you know Hannah had her baby?"

"I didn't."

His eyebrows furrowed together as she drew closer. "What's wrong?"

Her lips quivered as she blinked back tears.

"Come here." Closing the distance, he wrapped his arms around her. He pulled her against his chest, cupping the back of her head.

She nestled closer to him with tears streaming down her face. "My dad just died."

"Oh, Mac." His voice sounded hoarse as if her grief caused him pain. He tightened his hold—those strong, sturdy arms, making her feel protected.

"My mom blamed me for his death." Her words came out muffled against his shirt. "All I ever wanted was to see my mom happy. I was naïve to think she could be."

"No, you weren't. You're an amazing daughter."

"You really think so?"

"Of course. Most people wouldn't have tried to help them." He moved his hand from her hair and gently rubbed her back. "Have you ever considered that you were meant to be their daughter?"

Sniffling, she pulled back to look up at him. "What do you mean?"

He wiped away her tears with his thumb. "Maybe you were supposed to be theirs, to love them despite all of their mistakes."

"I don't know about that."

"You might not right now, but one day, you'll see that I'm right."

She nodded. Could it be true? Part of her wanted it to be, to make sense of her childhood. But then again, maybe some things in this world could never be explained. Like Lynn staying married to Jack despite his abuse. Or her parents not wanting custody of her. Or Charlie's accident and losing Ally.

She shuddered as the last of her tears fell down her cheeks. She couldn't tell Charlie that he might be wrong. He sounded so sure of himself. "I hope you're right."

A hint of a smile graced his lips. "I'm always right."

She returned a small smile and turned her head toward the nursery. "So Hannah had her baby?"

He nodded, a light returning to his eyes. "Yeah. Do you want to see him?" He dropped his arms to his sides and stepped closer to the window.

She followed his gaze to the sleeping babies in the nursery, her arms feeling cold without his touch. "Which one is he?"

He pointed to a baby on the left. "Benjamin's right there."

She stepped closer and pressed her palm against the window. Wrapped in a blue blanket, Benjamin's eyelids fluttered open as he sucked on a green pacifier. His little face was tinged pink, like the color of the sky after a rain. "He's precious."

"I know." Charlie stood transfixed as he peered into the window and waved at the baby, wiggling his fingers.

Her heart swelled. Not only would he become a good uncle, but a good dad someday. Maybe someone like him could teach his kids to learn from their mistakes. To move past their pain. To make their lives better.

"I can't wait to take Ben to baseball games and Maple Valley festivals. He's going to love them," Charlie said.

Her hopes lifted. "So you might consider staying here, then?"

He glanced at her and grinned before turning back to Ben. "I'm definitely thinking about it."

She stepped back to study his profile. She'd seen that passionate look in his eyes before but when?

She cupped a hand over her mouth. The night of the accident.

His eyes had been filled with the same heartfelt intensity, tainted with anguish. She'd assumed it was guilt: Ally's death, losing his job, ruining his family's prestigious status, but she was wrong.

Seeing that look again, she knew with certainty there was more than guilt. Charlie had truly loved Ally. And now he loved Ben.

All this time she'd been fooling herself. She'd closed

herself off to the possibility of love by holding back, by guarding her heart so she wouldn't have to expect her parents, or anyone else, to love her.

But maybe she'd been wrong. What if love really did exist?

Chapter 14

CHARLIE WALKED INTO Hannah's hospital room, feeling torn. If only he could be in two places at once. Mac needed his support right now, but so did Hannah. So far, Daniel hadn't shown up to the hospital. When Mac heard this, she'd insisted on leaving so he could spend time with his family. She was an amazing woman. He'd never met anyone who was as willing to care for other people, even when they didn't want it.

Hannah opened her eyes as he walked farther into the room. After ten hours of labor, no doubt she was groggy and sore.

"Do you need anything?" he asked.

"No, I just needed some rest. I feel much better after that nap." She clicked a button on the side of her bed. A low drumming noise brought the bed to life as it inclined, raising Hannah to an upright sitting position. "Did you see Benjamin in the nursery?"

"Yeah." He walked to the window and leaned against the ledge, early morning sunlight pouring in to warm his skin. "He's one handsome kid."

"I think so, but then again, I'm biased."

He looked up as Daniel approached the doorway, wearing jeans and a wrinkled dress shirt from the night before. His unkempt hair lay matted across his forehead. "Hey."

"Where were you?" Hannah's voice trembled.

"I was downstairs asleep in the guest room. I got home late and I didn't want to wake you. I'm sorry I missed your calls." He shuffled into the room and stopped beside the bed, kissing Hannah on the cheek. He handed her a large blue gift bag on the bed. "Look what I brought Ben."

"Is this supposed to make up for not being here for the birth of your son?"

"I said I'm sorry." He blinked back the moisture building in his bloodshot eyes. "I actually bought this to make up for not painting Ben's room. I know you wanted it done before he was born."

Charlie groaned. He hadn't finished helping Hannah paint Ben's room yet, either.

Hannah shrugged. "There's nothing we can do about it now. No one planned on me delivering three weeks early."

She tipped the bag and peeked inside. Carefully pulling out the first gift, she unwrapped it to find a box of baby bottles. Next, she pulled out a navy bib with yellow trucks on it and held it up for them to see. "This is adorable."

"I thought you'd like it." Daniel pulled a chair up next to her bed.

"My parents are on their way," Hannah said. "I tried calling yours, but they didn't answer. I'm worried that we won't get ahold of them, at least for a week. They're still on their white-water rafting trip in the mountains. It's not like they were expecting us to call this soon."

"Oh, yeah, that's right." Charlie scratched his head. Hopefully, his parents would have phone service in the mountains. "I'm sure they'll call back soon."

Hannah nodded and returned her attention to the presents. She laid an assortment of newborn outfits on the bed. "Your dad is going to love the onesie with the picture of a tie on it. Ben will look like a little business executive."

"I thought so, too." Daniel turned to Charlie, smirking. "Mom and Dad are excited to *finally* be grandparents." His words hung in the room like a heavy fog.

Charlie scoffed. He didn't need Daniel to remind him. It had been running through his mind all morning.

"Knock, knock." The nurse breezed into the room with Benjamin wrapped snugly in a blue blanket. "Do you want to hold him, Dad?"

"Of course."

"We recommend skin-to-skin contact between parents and baby. Do you want to take off your shirt and I'll place Ben next to your chest?" the nurse asked.

"Sure." Daniel stood and unbuttoned his shirt, then tossed it on the couch.

The nurse transferred Ben into Daniel's outstretched arms. She stood there for a while, eyeing Daniel cautiously. Finally, she said, "Let me know if you need anything," before leaving the room.

Pressing his son close, Daniel ran a finger over Ben's face. "He's perfect."

Hannah reached for her phone, snapping a picture.

"He'll be a great athlete, just like me," said Daniel.

Charlie moved away from the window and stood near Daniel, reaching for one of Ben's hands. Little fingers curled over his. "Between the two of us, he might be good at sports and at school."

Daniel scowled. "I thought you were leaving after your parole."

Charlie's smile faded. Now that Ben was born, he couldn't wait to spend more time with his nephew. To babysit him and take care of him when Hannah needed a break. He'd be the cool uncle who fed Ben candy and let him stay up later than his bedtime. For the first time since moving back to Maple Valley, he saw the potential for staying here. "I might stick around after all."

Daniel looked at him. "Let's get one thing straight. I

don't want you spending a lot of time around my kid."

Charlie flinched as if he'd been burned, his excitement flickering like a fading candle. "Why not?"

"Don't do this right now," Hannah sputtered. "We just had Benjamin. Let's all get along."

"If you live here, do you honestly think Ben will grow up without knowing that you went to prison?" Daniel asked.

Charlie stared at his brother. "No, but that won't matter to Ben when I take him to baseball games and teach him how to throw a football." The words escaped before he had a chance to consider what he'd just said. But now the words resonated inside of him and a sense of relief took hold, shaking him to the very core. He needed to stop living like a wounded man of the past and see life like a child would—focusing on the present, for better or for worse.

"It'll matter." Daniel walked to the bed and handed Ben to Hannah. Turning around, he crossed his arms and stood beside the bed, his legs shoulder width apart. "I don't want you to teach my son anything."

Charlie grimaced. "Well, at least I didn't become the owner of Charger's by default."

Daniel's eyes flashed with anger as he turned to Hannah. "You told him?"

She was talking softly to the swaddled baby in her lap. Looking up, she grew quiet and her lips trembled. "I didn't mean to; it just came out."

Daniel grabbed his wrinkled shirt, shoving his arms through the sleeves as he turned back to Charlie. "I deserve ownership. I'm the oldest."

"So what? Dad couldn't trust you to run the business."

"I'm done with you." Daniel held up his hands, tapping his fingers as he counted off the list of annoyances. "You live at my house, you eat my food, and you're with my wife all the time. If I didn't know any better, I'd say you have feelings for her."

"What? I think of Hannah as a *sister*. Maybe if you were home more, you'd know that."

"I'm not home because I'm working." Daniel yanked both sides of his shirt across his chest, cramming the buttons into place. He missed a couple of holes at the bottom, his shirt hanging unevenly above his jeans. "Just admit it: for the first time in your life, you're jealous of me."

Charlie shook his head.

Daniel took a step closer. "You're a pathetic dog walker working for minimum wage."

"Pathetic, huh? What's pathetic is that you're arguing with me when you could be holding your newborn son."

Daniel inched closer, standing directly in front of Charlie.

Counting to ten, he took deep, steadying breaths as

he clenched and unclenched his fists. "Get away from me."

"Or what?"

His fingernails bit into his palms. He should leave before the situation got out of hand, before he did something he regretted.

Daniel's arms flung forward, his hands slamming into Charlie's chest.

Charlie stumbled, but regained his balance. He planted both feet, unwilling to back down. Daniel had crossed the line and he wasn't going to put up with his brother's insults any longer. Pulling back his arm, he aimed a punch at his brother's cheek.

"Stop!" Hannah yelled.

Smirking, Daniel pushed Charlie to the floor and jumped on top of him.

Pain seared through the back of his head as it slammed into the floor. He blinked, trying to clear his vision. "You're. Going. To. Regret. This."

Daniel laughed. All of his weight pressed on Charlie as Daniel jabbed at his face.

With one swift movement, Charlie turned his body to the side and pushed Daniel off of him. He pulled back his arm. Ben's wail pierced the room as footsteps hustled inside.

He turned to find a nurse standing in the doorway, her face stricken with worry. She eyed the two of them, backing out into the hallway. "Someone call security!"

CHARLIE TRACED THE tender skin around his eye. Why had he let Daniel get to him? He should have left the hospital room before things got heated. He should have listened to Hannah's pleas. But now it was too late. Too late to go back and make a different choice, once again.

Wincing, he dropped his hand and slammed it against the jail bars. What had he been thinking? If the judge decided he was at fault for the fight, he'd go back to prison.

He lowered his head against the bars. What would Mac think of him now? He hated the thought of disappointing her. Besides the possibility of going back to prison, she was all he'd been thinking about. Holding her in his arms at the hospital, feeling her heart beat against his. She'd looked so sad and vulnerable, and he'd wanted nothing more than to scoop her up and take her home, away from the hospital. They could've spent the day cuddling on the couch, watching movies, and … He stopped his thoughts before they could go any further. *Not happening* he reminded himself.

Especially if he got incarcerated again.

One of the guards strolled over to his cell and unlocked the door, glancing at Charlie. "You have a visitor."

Charlie walked to the open door and stopped in front of the guard. "Who is it?"

"Your parole officer."

Cracking his knuckles, he followed the guard into a small room with a table and two chairs. Mac sat at the table, her lips drawn into a thin line.

He dropped down into the empty chair, rubbing the tension out of his neck. His gut soured at her reaction. She didn't deserve to be in jail, visiting him when she had so much else going on.

"What happened?" she asked.

"Daniel and I got into an argument and then he started punching me."

"Did you punch him back?"

"No. I pulled him off of me just as the nurse came into the room."

She leaned forward, resting her elbows on the table. Her fingers formed a steeple under her chin. "The nurse saw you getting ready to punch Daniel."

"I know, but I didn't."

Sighing, Mac shook her head. "How could you do this?"

He slumped back against the hard, plastic chair. "I wasn't thinking."

"No, you definitely weren't." Her voice was drenched in disappointment.

"Look, I messed up. I'm sorry."

"You don't have to apologize to me."

"Yes, I do." He looked directly in her eyes, his chest aching. "After everything that happened with your parents, you don't need this."

Her lips parted as she dropped her hands to the table. "You might be going back to prison, and you're worried about me?"

"Of course." Charlie leaned forward, reaching for her hands. His thumb caressed the inside of her palms. He shouldn't be touching her like this, especially in front of the guard, but she had to know how sorry he was for being a burden to her.

Mac stared at him for a moment, then pulled her hands away. As she stood, he swallowed hard, wishing she would sit back down and let him hold her hands again. But the look on her face made it clear she wasn't in the mood to be touched.

She paced across the tiny room. "You can't sweet talk your way out of this. I have no control over whether you go to prison."

"What are you talking about?"

"I know I joked about this, but I'm beginning to think it's true—you're just flattering me so you can get your parole over faster."

"Is it so hard for you to believe that I might care about you?"

Mac stopped pacing. His admission seemed to have bothered her. She glanced at the guard before looking back at Charlie. "I better go."

He stood up as she walked to the door and twisted the knob. "Wait."

She turned around, black strands falling across her shoulders. "What?"

"Why did you come?"

"I wanted to make sure you were okay," she said quietly.

A sad smile tugged at his lips. "Thank you."

She nodded and opened the door.

"Mac? One more question." As she stared at him expectantly, he imagined walking across the room and wrapping his arms around her, like he'd done at the hospital.

"What is it?"

"Do you think I'll go back to prison?"

Her shoulders wilted. "I don't know."

Charlie pinched the back of his neck. Now, he had to wait and see what the judge would decide. The thought left his stomach in turmoil. Would he have to spend more time in prison?

Not only would he be stuck behind bars, but he wouldn't see Ben or Mac anymore. In fact, Mac might have already chosen not to have anything to do with him.

A heavy ache filled his chest.

Chapter 15

THUNDER REVERBERATED THROUGH the Canine Palace. A high-pitched wail came from the backroom, followed by a chorus of barking and whining.

Charlie stepped into the backroom to check on the dogs. If the storm didn't let up soon, none of the dogs would get their walks today.

The smell of poop permeated the room. He moved the dogs into clean kennels, then grabbed rags and cleaner and dropped to his hands and knees. As he scrubbed, Ray's theory came back all too quickly. *Some people need to pick up poop. It gives them wisdom.*

He scrubbed harder. He deserved this task today, but at least he wasn't in jail anymore. The judge had determined he wasn't in violation of his parole since he'd never actually hit Daniel.

He finished cleaning and left the backroom to find Ray. "Since it's still raining, do you want me to help with the books?"

Ray slouched behind the register. His head was in his

hands as he rested his elbows on the counter. White tufts of hair stuck between his thick fingers.

Charlie furrowed his eyebrows. "Are you all right?"

Ray dropped his hands. His hair jutted out at odd angles. "It's my wife's birthday."

"Oh." He walked to the counter and leaned against it. "If you want, I can take care of the store, so you can spend the day with her."

"No, I can't." Ray stared at the grooming station, a faraway look in his eyes. "She, uh, she passed away a few years ago."

"I'm sorry to hear that," he said in a quiet tone.

"She died the same week you went to prison. I remember because I had a news reporter following me around for days."

Charlie scratched his head. "For an obituary?"

"No. She was a columnist for the *Maple Valley Tribune*. The reporter wanted to write an article about her death. It was supposed to be on the front page." Ray took off his glasses and wiped them on his shirt. Wrinkles creased the skin beneath his tired eyes. "I'm glad it never got published."

"Why?"

"I didn't want to make her death more public than it already was." He paused and looked at Charlie, a painful expression crossing his face. "She committed suicide."

His eyes widened. The happy, energetic woman he'd

seen at football games had taken her own life? It didn't seem possible.

He took a closer look at Ray as the old man slid his glasses back on top of his nose. No wonder he'd stopped coaching and wanted to have a job where he wasn't in the limelight anymore. "What happened to the article?"

"It was given to me and never put in the paper."

"How did you convince the reporter?"

Ray ran a hand over his beard. "I didn't have to. Your accident occurred and your story made the front page instead."

He stiffened, thinking back to the day he'd first met Ray. "Is that why you hired me? You thought you owed me something?"

"No, that's not why I hired you." Sighing, he straightened his posture and gave Charlie a serious look. "I was waiting to tell you this, but I guess now is as good a time as any."

"Tell me what?"

"You're a good employee."

"Thanks."

Ray leaned forward, setting his forearms above the counter. "You work extra hours, I never have to tell you what to do, and you've given me some great ideas to increase revenue." He gave Charlie an earnest look. "Would you consider being a part owner with me for the next couple of years, with the intent of completely owning the shop after I retire?"

His mouth hung open. "I, uh … I don't know what to say."

"I figured this would be the perfect scenario. You could work with animals and help with the store's finances."

"This means more to me than you'll ever know, but …" What would Ray say when he found out about the fight with Daniel? Would he still want Charlie to be a part owner? He opened his mouth to say something but he just stuttered, "Um, I really don't … " Ray walked around the counter and pulled Charlie into a hug, his words becoming muffled against the old man's shoulder.

"Great. I'll take that as a yes." As they stepped out of the embrace, Ray patted Charlie's shoulder. "Oh, and one more thing. I don't know where your bruises came from, but try not to come in here looking like the hooligan that some people think you are."

DANIEL ROLLED OVER in bed and blinked through the sunlight to glance at the alarm clock. Groaning, he pulled the covers over his head and closed his eyes. Lately, it was hard to find the will to get out of bed. Every morning he woke up, reality threatened to pull him under. Charlie wasn't going back to prison.

He shouldn't have let his anger get the best of him and punched Charlie first. Why did everything always work out perfectly for his brother? According to Hannah, he was on his way to becoming the owner of the Canine Palace. And as for women? Not a problem. Even his pretty little parole officer was attracted to him. That was obvious from the hug Daniel had seen on his way to the hospital gift shop. This wasn't supposed to happen. Charlie was supposed to be struggling, not thriving.

"Wake up." Hannah's voice carried from the doorway.

He sat up in bed, rubbing the sleep out of his eyes.

Hannah walked to the side of the bed, shifting her weight from side to side as she held Ben against her chest. Loose strands of hair fell across her forehead. "Will you take Ben for a while? I want to take a shower."

He opened his mouth and shut it. He cared about Ben more than anything, but having an infant was hard. He just needed a few more hours of sleep, and yet, he couldn't tell Hannah that. Not when she was the one getting up every few hours and breastfeeding.

She yanked the covers off of him. "Do you realize Charlie's taken care of Ben more than you have?"

Letting out a low growl, he swung his legs over the side of the bed. "How dare you!"

"It's true." She lowered Ben into his arms and put

her hands on her hips. "He's changed diapers, he's helped me in the middle of the night, he's—"

"Stop." His command sliced through the room. "I don't want to hear about how great you think *my brother* is."

She lifted her chin, her gaze unwavering. "Look, I know it's a sensitive subject for you, but you have to stop being jealous of your brother. It's not healthy."

"Maybe I wouldn't be if people like you didn't remind me how much better he is than me." Daniel clenched his teeth, resentment spreading across his chest.

She rubbed her temples. "That's not what I was trying to say."

"Yes, it was." He waited for her to respond, to explain her reasoning, but she offered nothing. He shook his head and marched past her, heading down the stairs. He needed to get as far away as possible from her before he said something he regretted. He was sick and tired of being compared to Charlie and falling short. No matter what he did, he was never good enough—first in his parents' eyes and now Hannah's.

The doorbell rang as his foot touched the bottom stair. Who could be here now? It seemed like the whole town had brought over meals already. Not that he was complaining.

"I'll get it." Charlie's voice came from the entryway. The door swooshed open, sending hot air up the staircase. "Hey, Mac."

Clutching Ben close to his chest, Daniel darted off the steps and leaned against a wall in the kitchen, hidden from view. What did the parole officer want?

"Come on in." Charlie widened the door.

"I can't. I have to leave soon, but I wanted to talk to you," Mac said.

"What's up?" Charlie asked.

"I've been wanting to ask you … Did the fight with your brother start because you confronted him about cheating?"

Daniel gritted his teeth to keep from yelling. If he weren't holding Ben, his hand would be in the wall. Mac had told Charlie he'd been cheating, which wasn't true. But if Charlie believed her, he'd probably told Hannah. No wonder Hannah had been so grouchy with him.

"The fight started because Daniel doesn't want me around Ben." Charlie sounded angry. "He thinks I'm a bad influence."

"Seriously?"

Daniel sneered. At least Charlie was still mad. But now what? If he couldn't provoke Charlie to fight him, how could he cause his brother to go to prison again?

"Maybe Daniel will change his mind," Mac said.

"I doubt it."

"I'm glad you didn't fight your brother. I'm sure it was hard. Even *I* might have punched him."

Daniel narrowed his eyes as Charlie laughed.

They spoke for a few minutes before Mac had to go.

The door clicked shut. Daniel clenched his jaw. Maybe he could get Charlie sent back to prison using the parole officer. His hopes lifted a little, diminishing some of his fury. Why hadn't he thought of this before now? It would be tricky, but he could do it.

Charlie strode into the kitchen, a smile plastered across his self-righteous face. Catching sight of Daniel, his brother stood still. "Were you listening to my conversation?"

"Nope." Daniel moved away from the wall and opened the fridge, supporting Ben with one arm. He took out a container of orange juice. Tilting his head back, he took a swig. Three years ago, Plan A had worked better than expected. No doubt Plan B would be just as successful. He gulped the rest of his juice and wiped his mouth with the back of his hand. Now, he just needed the guts to go through with it.

Chapter 16

ORANGE AND PINK hues smeared across the sky like a watercolor painting. The sun rose on the horizon and peeked between pine trees scattered across the expanse of land. A cool breeze glided through a pair of rusty iron gates at the entrance of Resting Haven Cemetery.

Charlie walked through the gates and looked down at Jackson. "Let's go, boy."

Clutching a bouquet of yellow roses, he strode toward the pond. The location of Ally's grave couldn't be better. Hopefully, the people who walked by the pond also happened to notice it. She deserved to be remembered and that's exactly what he intended to do after today.

It was time to let her go, so he could move on. He would hold on to the memories, and let go of the guilt. He was certain that this was the right choice. He couldn't remain stuck in the past, regretting his decisions forever. What kind of life would that be? He might as well be in prison, confined to a life without friends or family.

He stopped at the pond, signaling for Jackson to heel. The dog sat down in the grass and stared at two white swans gliding over the water side by side. The birds looked peaceful in their own little world, unaware of the tragedies that brought visitors to their home.

A group of mallards congregated under a willow tree and jumped into the pond, paddling over to him with their beaks hungrily opened for food. Charlie glanced at the bouquet in his hands. He had nothing to give the birds, only the flowers for Ally. He turned and made his way toward her grave.

When he saw it, he dropped to his knees. The muddy grass sank beneath his weight as he stared at her name. Allyson Marie Grimm. He leaned over and traced the letters with his fingers. His chest constricted. If only he could touch her face one more time, feeling her soft skin under his fingers instead of the cold, hard grave.

Blinking, he set the roses on the grass. "I miss you so much."

He pounded his fist into the grass. "I should have listened to you. You didn't deserve to die because of my stupid choices. I just wanted our anniversary to be special." He grabbed a fistful of grass. "That night I'd planned on telling you that I was ready to have kids. I couldn't wait to see the look on your face."

He hunched forward with a heavy heart and pressed his forehead against her grave. Sobs wracked his body. Ally would've been a great mother. His stomach coiled. How selfish he'd been. He should have made his family his first priority. Not work.

Lifting his head from the gravestone, he took a shaky breath. "I'll never stop loving you. Even if … I'm falling for someone else."

He sat up and leaned against a nearby tree. Jackson stepped into his lap and licked his shaking hands before curling into a ball. Charlie stroked the dog's back and looked down at Ally's grave. An unexpected weight lifted off his chest.

He couldn't deny his feelings any longer. He was falling for Mac and couldn't imagine his life without her. He liked being with her more than anyone else in the world. She was confident, unselfish, beautiful, and when she let her guard down, she was a lot of fun.

He shouldn't tell her, not while she was his parole officer. But he knew all too well that life could be cut short. If he died tomorrow, it wouldn't matter if he broke the rules against parole officer-client relationships and told her the truth. His life was back on track because of her encouragement. He couldn't stop thinking about her. He wanted to be more than her client.

And yet, a seed of doubt planted inside his mind. Mac might not feel the same way. And even if she did, could he let her risk her career for him?

CHARLIE STOCKED THE display case with more dog cookies and brownies. No doubt Marion and Norma would be in to pick up goodies for Kasi and Maddie. The schedule showed that both dogs had birthdays tomorrow.

The doorbells jingled as the door swooshed open and Mac walked inside, scraping her heels against the *Wipe Your Paws* mat. She searched his face, her eyes filling with compassion. "It looks like your bruises are starting to fade."

His heart picked up speed as he walked in front of the display case. Leaning against it, he smiled and raised an eyebrow. "And I was just beginning to like them. I think they made me look more rugged, don't you?"

Mac cleared her throat. "I have something I'd like to discuss with you."

"All business today, huh?"

She paced in front of him, looking determined. "You need to move out of Daniel's house immediately."

"I don't want to move out yet."

She continued pacing, her hands becoming animated. "Why?"

"Hannah needs help with Ben, and it will be easier to

help if I live there."

"That's really nice, but what if Daniel provokes you again?"

He crossed his arms. "Trust me. I can handle it next time."

Mac stopped moving and a strand of ebony hair fell in front of her face. "How do you know that?"

"I went to the cemetery to visit Ally, and I apologized for everything." He looked into her beautiful blue eyes. "I don't want to mess up everything I have going for me, and I'm ready to move on."

She gave him a sad smile. "It sounds like that's what you needed to do all along."

"Yeah, I think it was." He walked over to her and placed the loose strand of hair behind her ear. Her cheeks reddened as he dropped his hand away from her face. "What happens when my parole is over? Between us, I mean."

"There's no reason for me to see my clients after their paroles are over," she said with a sharp edge in her voice.

"You don't stay in contact with any of them?"

Red blotches appeared on her neck. She looked down at her feet, her chin almost touching her chest. "Not really."

Charlie took another step closer to her, his face inches away from hers. "What if I don't want this to be over?" His fingers grazed her chin, until he gently tipped her face up to his. Surprising him, she didn't move, looking up into his eyes. She wanted this as badly as he did.

His heart thudded loudly as he pulled her closer.

"Please, I can't … "

Closing his eyes, he leaned down, his open mouth cutting off her words for a soft, slow kiss. She tasted sweet, like honey. Heat flamed within him, and he had to hold everything back inside not to press her closer and savagely kiss her.

She set her hands on his chest, and for a moment, he thought she was going to slide her hands down his torso, but then she pushed hard, breaking off the kiss. "How dare you!" She took a step backward, her blue eyes blazing. "You know the rules."

He dropped his hands and a growl escaped his lips. "I don't know how you do it."

"Do what?"

"Deal with so many rules. You can't do this. I can't do that. I know my past, but there should be special circumstances. Don't you think? Ally's death was an accident."

Mac stood as rigid as a stone. "It doesn't work that way. The rules are the same for everyone."

"People deserve second chances."

"You're right." She looked at the floor before meeting his gaze. "But we can't control how we met. I'm your parole officer. Even after I'm not, nothing will ever erase that Ally . . . "

His stomach churned as he finished her sentence. "That Ally died while I was driving."

"Yes. People at work—"

He held her gaze, not willing to look away. "Would you get in trouble if you dated me after my parole is over?"

Mac walked backward toward the door. "Don't do this."

"Answer me."

"Warren would investigate to see if anything happened between us during your parole. And if they found out that you kissed me, well . . . " Her bottom lip quivered. "I could lose my job, a job I happen to love."

Her words stung, but now that he'd started this conversation, he wanted to get everything off of his chest. "I can guarantee you that loving your job can't even compare to loving another person."

"That's not fair. Who's to say what's more important?"

He shook his head, frustration boiling through his veins. "You're so caught up in your work that you'd never have time to know."

Mac swung the door open and paused in the entryway. "This can't happen again." She dashed outside without looking back. The doorbells jingled in her absence.

Charlie pounded his fist on top of the display case. He'd just ruined everything.

CLUTCHING HER GAS station cappuccino, Mac flung open the door to the main office. She had to talk to Jen. To tell her what happened and ask for her advice. Should she come clean and tell Warren everything?

Jen stood with her back to the entrance, a mane of curly red hair bouncing up and down as she slid mail into employees' cubbies. "Hey darlin'."

Mac slumped into a chair at Jen's desk and raised her cup up in greeting.

Jen frowned. "Are you okay?"

She fiddled with the cup, slicing her nail into the Styrofoam. Where to start? *I'm sorry. I've been lying to you. I do have feelings for Charlie, and just an hour ago, he kissed me.*

"Seriously, what's wrong?" The office filled with silence as Jen put the last bit of mail into a cubby and set her hand on her hip. "If you don't tell me what's wrong, I'm going to call Tucker and tell him that you'll go on a date with him."

She narrowed her eyes. "You will not."

The edges of Jen's glossy lips curled into a grin.

"There's the spunk I was looking for."

Mac shook her head, the start of a smile touching her own lips.

"So are you going to tell me, or what?"

She could tell Jen lots of things that would shock her. Like the chills she'd felt when Charlie had looked at her hungrily, as if she were the only woman left in the world. Or the warmth of his touch when he'd brought her body closer to his. Or the burning desperation she'd felt when he'd set his lips on hers. Even now, it made her breathless. She'd had to use all her willpower not to wrap her arms around his neck and kiss him back.

She stood up to face the waiting room, checking to make sure no one else was around. Not seeing anyone, she turned back to Jen. "Charlie kissed me."

Jen's mouth dropped open.

"Don't worry; I stopped him right away."

"What are you going to do now?"

"I don't know." Charlie was still her client. Where were they supposed to go from here? She couldn't pretend that the kiss never happened. Not a kiss like that. One that left her weak in the knees, making her insides tremble.

Jen sat down on top of her desk and squeezed Mac's hand. "I think you know what you should do."

Ugh. Jen was right. There was only one way to fix this problem. "I have to talk to Warren."

"You can't."

"Why not?"

"Warren already left for the conference."

Mac glanced up at the clock and jumped off the chair. The conference started in four hours. "I completely forgot. Tucker is probably wondering where I am. I was supposed to pick him up twenty minutes ago."

Swinging her purse over her shoulder, she dashed out of the office, reaching for her car keys.

With every step toward the parking lot, her stomach tightened. She'd have to wait to talk to Warren. Unfortunately, no amount of time could prepare her for what she had to say.

Chapter 17

MAC HOPPED OUT of her truck into the sweltering heat in front of the Lodge Hotel in Des Moines. Glancing up at the tall building, she tugged on her red dress shirt and pencil skirt, straightening out the wrinkles. "Let's get inside before we melt."

Opening the back of her truck, Tucker swung their luggage over his shoulders.

"I don't need you to carry my bag. I'm fully capable of doing it on my own."

"You've been in a bad mood since you picked me up." He scowled and dropped her duffle bag on the ground next to her feet. "You're the one who asked me to go to the conference, remember?"

Mac rolled her eyes and hustled toward the entrance. "This is why I wanted to go by myself," she mumbled.

"I can hear you." Tucker strode next to her and opened the door.

Conference attendees stood wall to wall in the lobby. Some were crowded around a buffet off to the side and some sat on couches talking. She pushed through the cluster of people, toward the curvy check-in line.

Stopping at the end of the line, Tucker glanced at the clock, then back at Mac. "After we check in, we'll have to hurry to our rooms. Our first session starts in twenty minutes."

"You're such a stickler."

"Someone's gotta keep you in line."

Mac tried to smile, but she couldn't. Her head throbbed. Partly because of the heat. Partly because of the crowd. Mainly because of what she was about to do.

She had to request that Charlie be taken off her caseload. She wasn't going to lose her job or the respect of her coworkers for Charlie.

No doubt Warren would advise her to be cautious, even when Charlie was no longer her client. For her professional image, Warren wouldn't want her to date someone with a criminal record. She would assure him that she planned on keeping her distance. Things with Charlie would be over as soon as he was off her caseload.

Charlie would probably hate her for making the request. He'd wish he had never met her. If only he knew how badly she'd wanted to kiss him back. Just thinking about it made her heart break. Its broken pieces lay scattered through her chest.

But when he wasn't her client anymore, her feelings would fade, just like they had with every other guy she'd dated. So what if he made her laugh? Who cared if she felt comfortable opening up to him about her childhood? She could find some other guy. Or no guy. That would be even better. She didn't need a man in her life. She'd been doing just fine on her own.

WEAVING THROUGH THE crowded banquet room, Mac made her way toward Tucker and Warren. Along the way, people glanced in her direction, waving. She smiled. This conference was just what she needed: two full days of listening to speakers talk about victims' rights, drug abuse, and leadership skills. Talking to other officers about the daily struggles and positive outcomes with clients was a good reminder of why she'd entered this profession and why she needed to talk to Warren. Tonight. After the awards ceremony, she'd take him aside and tell him everything.

She draped loose curls over the front of her dress and stopped at a white-clothed table near the front of the room. "Good evening."

Tucker adjusted his tie and eyed her from head to toe. "Wow, you look stunning."

"I agree," said Warren.

Blushing, she sat down at the table and unrolled her silverware. She needed to do something, anything, to distract her from the tidal wave of nausea coursing through her stomach. Now that Charlie had kissed her, she didn't deserve to win the Outstanding Correctional Worker award. How could she accept the award after kissing a client? Even if she hadn't initiated the kiss, she'd led Charlie to believe their close relationship was okay. Definitely not an outstanding action.

But it wasn't just the ceremony that had her stomach in knots. The conversation she needed to have with Warren loomed over her head like a heavy cloud.

On stage, the president of the association tapped the microphone with his finger. "Ladies and gentleman, thank you for coming to the Iowa Criminal Justice Awards Ceremony."

She clasped her shaky hands beneath the table. Warren would probably ask her why she wanted to request Charlie off of her caseload. Could she tell him the whole truth? She hadn't been upholding her professional boundaries. She'd opened up to Charlie. Befriended him. Fallen for him.

"The Outstanding Correctional Program Award goes to David Upton."

She clapped with shaky hands. She should tell the whole truth. It was the right thing to do.

"The Multicultural Issues Award goes to Chris Zehner."

Mac clapped, barely making noise with her sweaty

palms. As she clapped, she noticed Warren watching her.

"The Outstanding Victim Assistance Award goes to Julie Lillibridge."

Did Warren sense her nervousness? Her guilt?

"And finally, the Outstanding Correctional Worker Award goes to … "

She resisted the urge to close her eyes. *Please not me. Don't say my name.*

"MacKenna Christensen!"

Mac froze with dread. *No, no, no.*

Tucker nudged her arm. "Go up there and get your award."

She stood on shaky legs as Warren rose from his seat. People from every table applauded. Swallowing the lump in her throat, she hesitantly walked up to the stage. The president handed her a wooden plaque with her name engraved on a gold plate.

She glanced down at the plaque, heat flaming beneath her cheeks. Sure, she'd put in long hours, she'd worked hard, helped clients get their lives back on track, but she didn't deserve this award. Not after falling for Charlie.

The applause grew louder. She blinked back the moisture in her eyes and scanned the banquet room filled with people who believed she was a great parole officer and with coworkers who viewed her as a professional woman in corrections. They didn't know what she was hiding.

Pushing her emotions aside, she lifted the plaque and mouthed *thank you* to the crowd. A photographer on the side of the stage urged her to come near. Mac plastered a smile on her face, then walked back to the table.

Warren waddled over and wrapped her in a bear hug. "Great job, kiddo." The pride on his face was undeniable.

She sank down into her chair, barely able to focus on the rest of the ceremony. Several people were recognized for their years of service. A few older men gave retirement speeches.

Warren kept looking over at her, smiling. How was she supposed to tell him about Charlie now?

At the end of the ceremony, she shot out of her chair and strode across the large room. She couldn't stand around and let people congratulate her.

"Wait, Mac." Tucker followed her out of the banquet room and into the hallway. He gently gripped her arm and pulled her to a stop outside the stairway. "You forgot your plaque."

Her shoulders lowered. "Oh. Thanks."

Tucker furrowed his eyebrows. "What's going on?"

"I don't want to talk about it." She chewed on the inside of her cheek. "I need some fresh air."

Tucker nodded, a look of confusion still spread across his face. "I know where we can go. There's a great view of Des Moines from the rooftop."

"Okay." Anything sounded good, as long as they could get away from the other conference attendees.

She followed behind him, climbing the stairs two at a time. When there were no more stairs left to climb, he opened the door, and led her onto the roof.

She blinked, adjusting to the darkness.

He led her to the ledge of the building. "Isn't it beautiful?"

She leaned forward and cautiously peered over the side. The downtown area of Des Moines was ablaze with light. Music blared from nightclubs. Pedestrians strode across the street in front of cars and laughter echoed through the night. "The city is so awake and energized. Somehow, I feel exhausted just looking at it."

He frowned. "You just won the best award of your career and that's how you're feeling?"

She sat down, close to the ledge. "I don't deserve it."

"You've changed a lot of lives. I can't imagine anyone working harder than you."

"Yeah, well … "

Tucker crossed his arms. "Does this have something to do with Charlie Grimm?"

She sighed. "Yes."

"It always comes down to him."

"Not always." She pushed stray hairs away from her face. "Just lately."

"Listen, I've stayed quiet long enough." He sat down next to her, placing his hands behind him and leaning back. "You remember the night of the car accident differently than me. You think about the accident and imagine Charlie. I think about that night and imagine you."

He turned toward her, his bald head gleaming in the moonlight. "When I was filing the police report, all I could think about was you."

She bit her bottom lip. Tucker hadn't been focused when he'd been writing Charlie's accident report?

He reached for her hand and caressed her palm with his thumb. "I care about you. I should've told you sooner. But how could I have known that by the time I got around to telling you how I feel, your heart would already be taken?"

"That's not … " She let the rest of the sentence trail off, not willing to lie anymore.

"I know you have feelings for him. But just so you know, I like you too." Tucker leaned in and softly pressed his lips against hers. When he opened his mouth, hers followed. She waited for her heart to race like it had when Charlie kissed her, but nothing came.

MAC SAT ON the edge of her unmade bed. Her makeup,

hair dryer, and clothes lay in organized piles at the bottom of the bed, next to her open duffle bag. "Did Charlie tell you why?"

Warren shifted in his chair. Bright sunlight poured through the hotel room window, glimmering across his dark umber face. "No, he didn't."

"What did Charlie say exactly?"

"I haven't talked to him yet. I just listened to my voicemails this morning and before I called Charlie back, I wanted to come straight to you."

"Oh." That explained why Warren had showed up unannounced to her hotel room at nine in the morning still wearing his sweats and a Cubs hat. "So Charlie just asked to be taken off my caseload? He didn't say anything else?" Just saying the words out loud made her stomach twist in knots. Even though she'd planned on making the same request, it was an unexpected punch in her gut. Charlie must not want anything to do with her.

"He just made the request. That's it." Taking off his hat, Warren toyed with the well-worn bill. Without the cap covering his face, his narrowed eyes became noticeable. "Do you know why Charlie made the request?"

She glanced down at her hands, which were tucked between her legs. "I think so."

"Care to enlighten me?"

She met his gaze like a guilty prisoner. "Charlie kissed me." She waited for her supervisor to respond, but he just stared at her and his hat fell to the floor. Hating the silence, she continued. "I stopped him right away. I told him that it could never happen again."

Warren opened his mouth and shut it before finally regaining his composure. "There must be a reason Charlie thought kissing you would be okay."

She lowered her chin to her chest. She couldn't stand to see the look of disappointment crossing her supervisor's face. "Charlie and I … We grew close. Too close."

Pursing his lips, he picked up his hat and set it back on his head. "As I'm sure you know, this warrants an investigation." He stood and crossed his arms. "I'll expect you to be more specific tomorrow when I question you at the office." Shaking his head, he turned and trudged out of the hotel room.

She slumped back against the bed, covering her face with her hands. Her career could be over. Warren would surely ask Jen and Tucker about her relationship with Charlie and they would tell Warren the truth. She didn't blame her friends; it was the right thing to do.

Even with their testimonies, maybe she still had a chance to salvage her career. She'd stayed late after the curfew-check so she could meet Daniel and assess Charlie's living situation. She'd spent time with Charlie at Candy Galore because of the hailstorm. When Charlie had kissed her, she'd stopped it right away. She had a reasonable explanation for almost all of it. What she couldn't explain were her feelings.

A heavy weight sank to the pit of her stomach. She had to make a decision—admit her feelings for Charlie and risk losing her job, or deny her feelings and live a life wondering what could have been.

Chapter 18

PASSING OTHER OFFENDERS in the lobby, Charlie stopped in front of the desk to check in. Above the counter, Jen slid the window open and frowned at him. "You're here early. You'll have to wait. Robert, your new parole officer, is still meeting with another client."

He cleared his throat. "Actually, I'd like to see Mac first."

Twisting one of her big hoop earrings, Jen glared at him. "I don't think that's a good idea."

"I have something I want to tell her." Like apologizing to her for the kiss. For overstepping boundaries. He didn't want to jeopardize her career and harm another woman with his bad decisions. That was why he'd called Warren and made the request to be taken off her caseload.

"Can I give her a message instead?" Jen asked.

"No. I want to talk to her in person."

"You can't." Leaning forward, Jen kept her voice sharp but quiet. "She's in Warren's office right now being investigated."

His eyes grew wide. "Why?"

"I think you know why."

His heart squeezed. If Mac was being investigated, it was his fault. He glanced at the clock. His parole meeting with Robert started in fifteen minutes. He would meet with Robert, then wait for Mac. If he couldn't convince Jen, he could surely convince Mac to see him. He needed to talk to her now more than ever. Afterward, they could meet with Warren together and he could take full blame. She didn't deserve to lose her job because of him.

He moved to one of the empty lobby chairs and sat. He rested his elbows on his thighs, silently rehearsing what he was going to say to her—the kiss was entirely his fault. He'd misread her feelings. It was time to move on with his life. It was clear, concise, and to the point. She'd have to understand.

His chest ached at the thought of telling her. He didn't want to say good-bye, but what else could he do? He couldn't change her mind.

Mac walked into the lobby, her gaze resting on him. Her chest rose and fell. She quickly looked away and strode back down the hallway as if she hadn't seen him.

He jumped out of his chair, jogging toward her. "Mac, wait."

She spun on her heels and crossed her arms. "What do you want?"

"We need to talk. It's important." Leaning forward, he kept his tone low. "I promise that's all I want to do. Then I'll leave you alone."

She glanced warily at Jen before meeting his gaze. "Fine. But I have to keep my door open. We shouldn't be alone in my office where people can't see us."

"Okay." He followed her into her office. Two coffee cups sat on her desk. A jacket hung half off, half on the back of her chair. A stack of articles lay haphazardly on the floor next to the garbage can.

A picture on one of the papers caught his eye. He picked it up. It wasn't just any article; it was about his accident. Holding the paper up, he looked at her. "Why do you have these?"

"I can explain, but I think you should sit down."

"I'm fine standing." He couldn't sit right now. The sharpness of her tone was sending too much adrenaline pumping through his veins.

Mac twisted her hands together and slowly walked behind her desk. She never took her eyes off of the floor. "I printed these articles so I could look at the pictures."

"Why would you do that?"

She ran a hand through her hair. "Because I wanted to remember."

"Remember what?"

"Your accident."

Charlie sank into the chair, his eyebrows pinching

together.

"I saw it all. Officer Tucker and I were on our way to arrest one of my clients." She lowered into her chair and bit her bottom lip. "We were right behind you at the stoplight."

He tossed the paper on her desk. If she had witnessed his accident, she'd seen Ally's body. She'd seen the blood on his hands. The reckless, selfish person he'd tried to cover up with his dressy clothes, his haircut, and his job. He'd never fooled her for a second. "You should have told me this before now."

"I wanted to, but it never seemed like the right time."

"The right time? I asked you if the officer told you anything about my accident. You could've told me then."

"I know, but … "

He jumped up and leaned over her desk, close enough to see her lips trembling. "Tell me. What did you see?"

She looked down at her desk, her dark hair falling in front of her face. "Why does it matter?"

"Look at me." Charlie put a hand under her chin, lifting her face so her eyes met his. "It matters because you were there to see the horrific scene. The horrific scene that I caused."

"I know," she said softly.

Blood pounded in his head. His face grew hot. "I thought you were different. I thought you saw something in me that nobody else did. But if you saw the accident, all you saw in me was a criminal."

"I *did* think that." Her eyes watered. "But after getting to know you … Now I feel sorry for you. I know how much you cared about Ally."

He stepped away from her desk, clenching his teeth. He didn't want people feeling sorry for him, especially not Mac.

"After I realized how much you regretted your decisions, all I ever wanted was to help you."

"Help me, huh? Just like you wanted to *help* your parents with their alcohol addictions?"

She blinked back tears. "No, that's different."

"It doesn't sound like it. I was just a project for you, wasn't I? Some client you could add to your list after you changed my careless ways?"

If all she'd ever wanted was to help him, then he'd mistaken her feelings for him. Mac didn't care about him as an equal. She saw their relationship as a kind parole officer helping a wounded client. Even without restrictions, he was never going to be worthy of her.

She reached for his hand. "Charlie, you have it all wrong."

He yanked his arm away, his voice rising. "Oh yeah? Then tell me the truth. Do you have feelings for me?"

"I . . . "

His heart pounded in his chest as he waited for her to respond. Silence filled the room, except for the gentle *tick, tick, tick* of the clock.

"That's what I thought." He put his hands behind his head. How could he have been so stupid? A parole officer wouldn't have feelings for an offender.

Tears streamed down her face. "I *do* care about you."

He shook his head. What a fool he'd been. "I came to apologize to you for overstepping boundaries, so guess what? I'm sorry. But that's not the only thing I'm sorry for. I'm sorry I fell in love with you."

Her teary eyes grew wide. "What?"

"I know it's not what you wanted to hear, but it's the truth." He turned away from her and strode toward the door.

She stood up, pressing her fingertips into her desk. "Please, let me explain."

Jen rushed into the office, looking from him to Mac. "I came to check on you. I could hear your voices all the way down the hallway."

Frowning, Charlie slid past Jen and stepped into the hallway. He glanced at Mac, wanting to say more, but there was nothing left to say.

MAC STARED BEHIND Jen's shoulder where Charlie had just stood a minute ago. "I need to be alone."

Jen nodded and left, shutting the door behind her. Her shadow remained under the door for a few minutes before finally fading away.

Mac didn't move. Tears dropped from her chin to the articles scattered across the floor. Each tear wet the papers and permanently blurred the words into messy blobs of ink. She shoved the articles to the side.

She shouldn't have searched for them in the database, but she'd felt compelled to find them. After Charlie made the request to be taken off her caseload, she wanted to remind herself that he was a man she'd hated. A man who had made reckless decisions and caused his wife to die. But instead, she'd seen a different man. Not a killer. Not a careless husband. But a man who'd suffered.

She slunk to the floor, sitting in a cross-legged position and carefully picked up each paper, running a finger over a picture of Charlie clinging to Ally's lifeless body. Another image showed him kneeling on the ground, his hands in the air, reaching for Ally as the paramedics took her away.

She clutched the articles to her chest as the memories enveloped her into a cocoon of regret. She had forgotten the anguishing contortions of Charlie's face. He was so heartbroken, so lost, so … in love.

As she rocked back and forth, tears streamed down

her face. She could grab the Kleenex box sitting on her desk, but she wiped her tears with her quivering fingers instead.

Her heart ached with the shocking truth—she was in love with Charlie Grimm. He'd been the one to knock down her guarded walls. He'd been the one to open up her heart.

She should have told him how much he'd helped her understand what was really important in life. He'd gone to prison, learned to appreciate what he had, and stopped taking life for granted.

Prison had made him a different person. A better man. Instead of getting a prestigious, high-paying job that his dad would want him to get, he found a job he enjoyed. A job that most people would look down on, Charlie found fulfilling. He'd stopped caring about what other people thought and had started living his own life.

Mac broke into full-body weeping that knocked her to the floor. She curled over her bent knees, her head buried in her hands. A prolonged sob erupted into the silent, stuffy office. She would probably lose her job, and now she'd lost Charlie too.

Chapter 19

As the early morning sun peeked through the blinds, Daniel glanced at Hannah's still form. Lately, she'd been sleeping lighter because of the baby and he had to be careful. Gently rolling off the bed, he kneeled down and reached underneath, pulling out a shoebox. He opened the box with trembling hands and retrieved his recent purchase—a small pistol.

Clutching the gun, he moved to the closet and grabbed a hidden plastic sack filled with clothes. He removed a pair of tennis shoes that were far too big, cargo shorts, a T-shirt, and gloves. He yanked the T-shirt over his head, slipped the shorts on over his boxers, and slid the gloves in the pockets of the shorts.

Fully dressed, he placed the gun in his pocket as he tiptoed into Charlie's room. Charlie lay sound asleep with blankets strewn across his ankles. Daniel snatched Charlie's cell phone and added it to his bulging pockets. Crossing the hallway, he walked into Ben's room. He had to take Ben along. The baby could possibly start crying and wake up Hannah or Charlie. He couldn't take any chances. Not today. Lifting a sleeping Ben out of the crib, he crept down the stairs.

In the kitchen, he opened the fridge and found a half-empty bottle of brandy. Liquid courage. Grabbing the bottle, he tilted his head back and chugged the remains of the bottle. When he'd drained the last drop, he threw the empty container in the garbage.

Quietly going out the back door, he strode to the edge of the woods, pressing the much-too-big shoes into the mud. The police would surely notice his brother's shoe prints. And when he was done with all this, he'd throw Charlie's clothes in the garbage where the police would surely see the splattered blood. That should be enough evidence to convict his brother of the murder and send him back to prison for good.

Nervous adrenaline pumped through his veins. He stepped through a narrow opening in the trees, carefully holding Ben against his chest so his little face wouldn't get scraped.

He kept his senses alert, striding toward a large tree that was bent in half, the bark charred from where he'd lit it to start the forest fire. Without branches and leaves, the rising sun peeked through the opening, providing just enough light to see clearly.

Stopping, he pulled out Charlie's cell phone and texted Mac. *I need to talk to you. Meet me in Daniel's backyard.*

His hand shook as he slipped the phone back into his pocket. With Mac on her way, he couldn't turn back now. Part of him wanted to. He'd never imagined murdering someone with his own two hands, but he was getting desperate. As much as he didn't like to admit it, jealousy was eating away at him, ripping away his pride like a savage animal killing its prey. Everyone preferred Charlie instead of him. His parents. His wife. It would only be a matter of time before Ben liked Charlie better, too.

He couldn't take it anymore. He had to kill Mac and make sure Charlie was out of his life for good.

His heart beat wildly in his chest. He could do it. In the end, it would be worth it.

MAC FOLLOWED THE wraparound porch to the Grimm's backyard. She placed a hand on her forehead and scanned the expanse of land. The water in the hot tub lay stagnant. Fish swam in the man-made ponds, nibbling on food. A blue jay landed on one of the marble fountains. But no sign of Charlie. Why did he want to meet her in the backyard, anyway?

She walked to the door and knocked. Had Charlie forgiven her? If he hadn't, she must apologize for hiding her feelings from him. Tell him how much she cared. She didn't want to spend the rest of her life without him.

She knocked on the door again. No answer.

A baby's blood-curdling scream came from the woods. The blood rushed out of her face as the cries grew louder, piercing the quiet morning.

She bolted off the porch and ran toward the sounds, into the woods. Her feet sank into the wet, muddy ground as she dashed between low hanging tree branches that cut her skin.

Suddenly, the screams ceased, as if someone had muffled the baby's mouth. She stopped to listen, leaning against a large oak. Leaves rustled in the distance. She crept around the tree, scanning the woods for some sign of movement. Thick brush blocked her view.

A twig cracked behind her. "You're late."

Mac turned, gasping. Daniel stood a foot away. "Where's Ben? I heard a baby crying just a minute ago."

"Don't worry about Ben." Daniel shot forward and knocked her down, then grabbed her ankles.

She scrambled to stand, to get away from him. She kicked at his hands, but he was faster. He dragged her out into a small clearing. One hand covered her mouth as the other pulled her into a standing position with her back to him. A few feet in front of her Ben lay swaddled in a blanket on the ground squirming.

"What's going on?" She tried to keep her voice calm.

Daniel laughed as she shook beneath his grasp. "I knew you'd show up if *Charlie* asked you to."

She swallowed hard. "You're the one who left me the message?"

"Don't be disappointed. I thought we could enjoy a nice morning together."

"Where's Charlie?"

"Am I not good enough for you?" Daniel whispered in her ear. Brandy stained his breath.

Mac shuddered. She shouldn't have run into the woods alone. She should have called Tucker when she'd heard the scream and let the police handle it. Now she was in the middle of the woods, defenseless.

He pressed cold metal against her head. "If you really want Charlie to be here, call him. Get out your phone."

"I … I'm fine if it's just you and me."

"Get out your phone," he ordered.

Mac kept her hands locked in place. "I'm not calling him. I don't want you to shoot him."

"Oh, I'm not planning on shooting my brother."

"Then why do you have a gun?"

"You're not as smart as I thought you were." Daniel rubbed his lips over her ear. "I brought the gun for you."

"To kill me?" The words stuck to her mouth like sticky candy.

"Yes. I can already imagine what the headlines will say—'Parole Officer Killed by Angry Parolee.' Don't you think it sounds plausible?"

"You'll never get away with this." Tears welled up in her eyes. This couldn't be real. Any minute now she was going to wake up from this terrible nightmare.

"You messed with the wrong guy. This is what happens when you spread rumors."

"Spread rumors?"

"I never cheated on Hannah. But you told Charlie that I did."

Tears streamed down her face.

"Don't cry. If I shoot you right in the head, it'll be painless."

"Please, don't do this."

Branches from a nearby oak tree moved to the side. Daniel tensed and tightened his grasp on her while hiding the gun behind Mac's back. "Who's there?"

No one answered.

With Daniel distracted, she stepped forward and tried to yank her arms away from him, only to feel the muzzle of the gun pressed against her head again. "I wouldn't do that if I were you."

"You don't want to kill me."

"Oh, but I do. It's all going to work out. For me, at least." He gave a nervous laugh. "You wouldn't be my first victim."

Mac gulped. Daniel had killed someone else?

With his free hand, he brushed the hair off her forehead in a strangely tender gesture. "Poor Charlie. He'll be devastated when he finds out another woman he cares about is dead."

She gasped with the sudden realization. Charlie's car crash wasn't an accident. Somehow, Daniel had caused it to happen. Twisting, she fought to get out of Daniel's grasp. She needed to get away to prove Charlie's innocence. "You caused the crash."

Straightening, Daniel tightened his arms around her, making it difficult to breathe. "So, you are as smart as I thought you were. Not that you'll be able to tell anyone."

"But how did you … "

"How did I cause the car crash?" She could almost sense Daniel smiling. "For weeks, I worked on Charlie's BMW while he was at Charger's, wore down the brakes to almost nothing, and finally told him to go to a mechanic. I knew Charlie wouldn't get them fixed right away. And with his lead foot and a snowstorm on the way, the chance of Charlie getting into an accident was highly likely."

She opened and closed her mouth, trying to grasp Daniel's confession.

"Then I stuck an empty bottle of Jack Daniels in the back of his car."

Her mind reeled. So Charlie had been telling the truth. The empty bottle wasn't his. She should have known it all along and given him the benefit of the doubt. And now it was too late. Daniel could shoot her at any moment.

He tightened his grip on her. "Of course, the bottle couldn't be used as evidence. But I knew it would cause suspicion, in case the other events didn't go as planned."

"Like Ally dying?"

"Yeah. That was a little trickier. I tampered with the retractor on the passenger side seat belt, hoping it would fail. But even if someone else had died in the crash, that would've been fine. As long as Charlie went to prison for causing it."

"Why didn't you just kill him?" she asked as movement in the bushes caught her eye.

"Death is easy. Prison isn't. I wanted him to suffer."

"Why?" She kept her eyes on the bushes, waiting for more movement. Who was out there?

He pressed the gun harder against her head. "I couldn't let Charlie take ownership of Charger's. I wasn't going to live in my younger brother's shadow any longer."

Jackson dashed across the grass and jumped on Daniel's leg, clamping down with his teeth.

"Stupid mutt. Where did you come from?" He kicked at Jackson, sending the dog rolling to the ground.

"Let Mac go."

Her eyes widened. Charlie stepped in front of the bushes, crossing his arms over his broad chest. He looked like Superman as he moved toward them, his eyes flashing with immense anger.

Daniel shoved the muzzle of the gun against Mac's head. "How long have you been here?"

"Long enough to know the accident was a setup," Charlie said through clenched teeth.

"Don't come any closer or I'll shoot her."

Charlie snapped his fingers, sending Jackson to run at Daniel again. Jackson bit Daniel's leg and Daniel's grip loosened. She twisted her wrists and pulled away from Daniel just as Charlie hurled himself at his brother, pushing Daniel to the muddy ground.

While Daniel was distracted, she searched for the gun. Did he have it? Were they rolling on it? She had to find it so they could hold Daniel hostage until the police got here. Wait. No one had called the police. She slipped a sweaty palm inside her pocket, grabbed her phone, and dialed 9-1-1. When the dispatcher answered, her words spilled out. "I need help at Daniel Grimm's house. He has a gun. We're in the woods. Hurry!"

Charlie's voice filled the air. "All this time I blamed myself for Ally's death and it was your fault. What kind of sick and twisted person are you?"

Daniel shifted his weight to the side and pushed Charlie off of him, holding the gun in his hand. "Mom and Dad aren't coming home to realize their baby boy is still the prodigy they remember." He jumped up and stood over Charlie, pushing his shoe into Charlie's chest to hold him down. "It's over." Daniel raised his arm and pointed the gun at her head.

Mac stood still. She should move. Get out of the way. Run.

Jackson dashed over to Daniel and bit his ankle.

Daniel screamed and lifted his foot, giving Charlie just enough space to roll away and jump up off the ground. Daniel's eyes grew wide as he watched Charlie run toward Mac, but he quickly composed himself and aimed the gun at her head once again.

A shot sizzled through the air as a heavy weight crashed into her, slamming her into the ground. Searing pains erupted through her head. She blinked away the blackness, trying to see, but only noises remained—Jackson's whimpers, Charlie's groans, Daniel's screams, and a deafening boom that rattled her hearing.

Chapter 20

LATER THAT NIGHT, Charlie awoke to the sound of footsteps entering his hospital room. He tried to roll to his side to see who it was, but shooting pains shot through his shoulder, where a surgeon had removed the bullet hours ago. He sucked in a rapid breath, waiting for the sharp stinging to subside.

Hannah leaned over the bed, holding Ben in her arms. "Sorry, I didn't mean to wake you."

"It's okay." The sight of Hannah brought a mixture of disappointment and panic gripping at his chest. Where was Mac? Was she hurt? After he'd jumped in front of the bullet—preventing her from getting shot—he'd gone unconscious. Since getting to the hospital, he'd been in and out of consciousness, and he couldn't remember much.

She sank into a chair next to the bed, gently patting Ben's back. Her eyes filled with concern. "How are you feeling?"

"Let's just say I can't get enough pain meds." He

slowly turned his head toward her, wincing. "How are you?" He wanted to ask about Mac, but he cared about Hannah and knew she'd been through a rough day, too.

She stared at the baby in her arms, her gaze distant. "I still can't believe it."

"I know," he said in a quiet tone.

Tears slipped down her cheeks. "How stupid can I be? My husband is a murderer and I didn't realize it."

"You're not stupid. I've asked myself the same thing. But there is no way we could have known."

Hannah shook her head. "The even crazier thing is, I keep thinking, what am I supposed to do without him?"

He gave her a sad smile. "When I lost Ally, I thought it was the end of the world. And for a while, it was."

She looked up from Ben, her eyes hopeful. "And now?"

"I still miss her, but I'm starting to look forward to the future." The longer their conversation went on, the more his panic grew. He could only appease his sister-in-law for so long before he asked about Mac.

Hannah squeezed his hand. "I'm so glad you're okay. If that bullet had hit your chest instead of your shoulder … "

He grimaced. "I try not to think about it."

She nodded, a slight smile playing across her face. "Mac's a lucky woman. You saved her life."

His head jerked up, sending a jolt of pain through

his shoulder. “So she’s okay?”

Hannah’s eyebrows drew together. “Yeah, she’s got a few scratches, but other than that, she’s fine. I thought you knew. She’s been in your room almost all day.”

Relief flooded through him. He’d been worried for nothing. She was alive. But now that he knew she was okay, he had other concerns. “Where is she?”

“In the cafeteria, getting some coffee. She plans on staying with you all night.”

His eyes widened. “She does?”

“Why do you look so surprised?” Her smile turned into a smirk. “You’re acting like you don’t know how Mac feels about you.”

In the silence, Hannah shook her head. “Seriously, Charlie? She’s crazy about you.”

A wide grin stretched across his face. He hadn’t misread her feelings after all.

CHARLIE RUSHED THROUGH the hospital doors out into the warm, summer day.

Mac ran toward him, her black, silky hair swaying across her shoulders. She flung her arms around his neck and wrapped her legs around his waist.

Chuckling, Charlie held her close and kissed her forehead. “Hey you. Thanks for picking me up.”

"I really didn't want to, but I figured it was the nice thing to do." She gave him a teasing grin.

"Are you trying to get under my skin?"

"I learned from the very best."

"You know me so well." He lowered her to the ground and glanced at her truck, parked near the curb. "Do you mind if I drive?"

Her eyebrows rose. "Really?"

"Yeah, I have somewhere I'd like to take you."

"Okay." She gave him the keys, her hand lingering over his. "Where are we going?"

"Just get in." He opened the door for her and took a seat behind the wheel. His hand shook as he turned the key in the ignition. The engine roared to life, and his Adam's apple bobbed up and down.

Mac laid a hand over his, rubbing her thumb against his skin. Her eyes filled with understanding. "I trust you."

"Thanks." His eyes met hers before he pushed the gas pedal, driving them out of the parking lot.

"I like your parents," Mac said.

"You do?"

"They're nice. A little hoity-toity, but they're definitely concerned about you." She laughed. "They aren't quite sure what to think of me, though."

Charlie turned out of the parking lot and drove down the street at a slow pace, his gaze focused on the road. "They'll come around."

"They're probably wondering why a parole officer is still hanging around their son."

"I'm still wondering about that, too."

She winked. "I think you know."

Gripping the steering wheel, he turned onto Ashmend Road and pulled over in front of the four-way stop, where they'd danced in the street.

Mac wrinkled her nose. "What are we doing here?"

He walked around the bed of the truck and stopped on the sidewalk, opening the door for her. He waited until she stood on the sidewalk before he explained. "I thought this would be the perfect place to tell you that I'm not running from my past anymore."

She blinked back the moisture building in her eyes. "I'm really glad to hear that."

He took a step toward her, breaking the distance between them. His heart beat wildly as she looked up at him, her gaze resting on his lips. He could finally kiss her without risking her job. Most of his charges had been dropped. He shouldn't have gone to prison, so Warren had discharged him from parole and stopped the investigation on her.

He leaned down, his eyes devouring her face before he lifted her off the sidewalk, bringing her hard against his chest. She stood on her tiptoes and wrapped her arms around his neck. Their lips met, electricity binding their mouths. She reached into the depths of his hair as his tongue sought hers, kissing her without guilt, without worrying about broken rules or offenses.

Breathing heavily, he let go of her waist. She kept her hands draped around his neck as she stood back on the sidewalk. Their gazes met, parted, and then met again. He pressed his lips against hers, the kiss taking on a softer tone.

When he finally pulled back again, her lips were moistened and slightly swollen. "I've been meaning to tell you that I'm glad you were at the accident."

She gave him a questioning look.

"Since you were there, I have nothing to hide from you."

"I've been meaning to tell you something, too." Mac put her hands on his chest. "I misjudged you. You're a better man than I gave you credit for."

"I've changed a lot. The person everyone used to know is gone. I don't even know who that person is anymore."

A warm smile spread across her face. "That's all right. I know the man you are now, and I like him a lot."

Grinning, he kissed her nose. "Oh yeah?"

"Okay, that's not entirely true." Standing on her tiptoes, Mac stood eye level with him, her lips brushing against his. "I'm actually in love with him."

Author's Note

Dear Reader,

Charlie Grimm was in my head for a long time before I wrote *Shackled Heart*. At first, he was simply a man who moved back to his hometown and didn't want to be there. Then I decided he must have done something he regretted immensely, something that would make *home* feel like a prison.

Enter MacKenna Christensen. It took a while to develop her backstory; she wasn't in my head like Charlie was. But I knew a parole officer would be the perfect career for her. She would have the opportunity to work with Charlie, despise him, then be able to look past his mistakes, and fall in love with him.

Just like Charlie was haunted by his irreversible mistakes, I was haunted by this story. After I wrote the first draft, someone I love went to prison. It was devastating. Suddenly, I felt much more connected to Mac. I had to live her character arc—experiencing her anger, compassion, and love.

I hope that Charlie and Mac's relationship shows the stilting power of guilt, the necessity of forgiveness, and the beauty of falling in love.

If you have a minute, please consider leaving a review. I thoroughly enjoy reading your thoughts and use your opinions to make each book better. Thank you in advance for leaving your opinion. It matters so much to me!

Love,
Crystal

Acknowledgments

Whew, time to wipe my brow! This novel went through at least three extensive revisions and multiple edits. Partly because the first draft of this story was written at five in the morning, while I was still an eighth-grade language arts teacher, and partly because of the extensive research I had to do.

It's taken so many years to write Charlie and Mac's story that I need to go back in time to thank all of the people who supported me from the very beginning and for all of the people who made Charlie and Mac's story the way it is today ...

Mom and Dad—We've been through a lot in the last few years. Our experiences were not anything I ever would've chosen for our family, but I appreciate the love you've shown to get us through. I hope that one day we can look back on these years and know we've all become better people because of it.

Handsome—Thank you for being one of the first people to read *Shackled Heart*. You've heard about Charlie and

Mac for so long, I think we both half-expect them to walk through our door as if they're our friends.

My two cutie pies—Landon, I was working on *Shackled Heart* the day I went into labor with you. What a special memory! Zoey—It's so fun to hear you run around the house saying, "*Shackled Heart*! Mommy's book." When you're older, I pray that both of you find someone who loves you no matter what happens in your lives.

Jen Tucker—Thank you for always believing in me. You made me feel like an author even when *Shackled Heart* was still sitting in my computer, and I hadn't published a word! Your curious questions about my books and writing always seem to come at the perfect moments.

Mandie Leytem, Jessica Pederson, Jenny Lauritsen, Kathy Cline, and Mike Schneck—You were my very first critique team. Oh how this novel has changed since you read that messy first draft! I'll never forget sitting with some of you at Bruegger's Bagels as you offered helpful advice. I hope you noticed: I kept "touché" in the book. I just had to.

Janice Boekhoff—This is the very first novel I exchanged with you. I had a blast eating lunch with you at Panera, brainstorming deeper, more suspenseful plot points. You've taught me so much!

Ben Hoffman, Lisa Kimbrough-Rodriguez, Nicole Thomason, Lyra VanLanduyt, Sarah Larsen, and Carly Errico—Thank you for your support!

Dad, Whitney Mann, Cynthia McIntosh, Peggy Urtz, and John Fayram—Thank you for taking the time to answer all of my questions about prison and parole. Your insight as corrections officers was invaluable.

My eighth-grade students—Your interest and questions about this book always gave me more motivation to finish it. It was an honor to be your teacher. Never forget to follow your dreams!

Crystal's Crew—I love getting your opinions! I appreciate every piece of advice and every post you make about my books. Thank you for sharing my stories with the world.

God—Thank you for the experiences you've given me to make this novel more realistic and meaningful.

Lastly, thank you, dear reader. You are such a blessing to me. Thank you for reading Mac and Charlie's story. I hope you enjoyed your time in Maple Valley.

Reader's Guide

1. At the beginning of the novel, Mac struggles to see past Charlie's mistakes. Would you have reacted similarly to her? Why or why not?
2. Charlie believes he deserves to pay for Ally's death and doesn't want to move on with his life. Why was it so hard for him to move on? Have you ever felt "stuck" in life?
3. Charlie and Mac both lost someone—Charlie lost his wife and Mac lost her dad. How were their responses different? Have you ever lost someone?
4. Warren often refers to Mac as his favorite workaholic. Why does Mac work so much? Is it healthy?
5. When did you catch on to Daniel's jealousy and his plan to send Charlie back to prison?
6. In what way does Jackson play a significant role in the book?
7. Charlie immediately falls in love with baby Benjamin and realizes he wants to be a part of his nephew's life.

He also realizes that Ben won't view him as a criminal; he'll just be Uncle Charlie. Why is this realization important for Charlie?

8. Mac doesn't like to talk about her childhood. Why does she finally open up to Charlie? Have you shared a secret about your past with someone? How did you feel after your conversation?
9. When Daniel divulges his plan to Mac and tells her that he's going to kill her, then frame Charlie, what was your reaction?
10. This novel explores the theme of loving someone despite their past mistakes. Why is forgiveness important? What makes forgiveness so hard?
11. Did you want Charlie to kiss Mac while he was still on parole? Why or why not?
12. What was your favorite moment between Mac and Charlie?

Read on for an excerpt of Book 2 of the Homeward Bound Series, *SHATTERED HEART.*

Chapter 1

AMANDA MEYERS BENT over the base of the bed, her gaze resting between her patient's spread legs. A dark head of hair blocked the birth canal. "I can see baby Emma."

Mac collapsed back onto a puffy pillow as she experienced another strong contraction. Screaming, she dug her fingernails into her husband's forearm. "I can't do this anymore."

"Yes, you can." Amanda sat up straighter and pushed back her shoulders, stretching out her muscles. A dull headache crept into her forehead, but she ignored it. After laboring for twelve hours, Mac needed Amanda's support now more than ever. "Are you ready to push again?"

Mac shook her head as a defeated look emerged in her heavily lidded eyes.

Amanda sent Mac an encouraging smile. Most of her patients at the Heartland Birth Center doubted their abilities at some point during labor, especially first-time moms like Mac. But the human body could perform miraculous feats. At the end, with their precious treasures cuddling on their chests, women often felt proud of how well their bodies had endured labor.

That was the best part about being a midwife—helping patients gain confidence in their physical abilities.

Mac leaned forward and expelled several quick breaths as another contraction started. "I want to push."

Amanda's chest swelled with pride. Mac was someone who had never wanted kids until she became an aunt. Seeing her transformation from no-way-I'll-never-be-a-mom to a waddling pregnant woman to now experiencing the last stage of labor was beautiful.

Mac's husband, Charlie, and one of the assistants grabbed Mac's bent legs.

"Whenever you're ready," said Amanda.

Mac let out a long, low grunt. Instead of moving, Emma's head stayed in the same position.

Amanda checked the fetal monitor. The heart rate had dropped from 130 to 120 beats per minute. Sudden drops in the heart rate weren't necessarily a cause for concern. Sometimes the umbilical cord could stretch and compress during labor, leading to a brief decrease in blood flow to the infant.

Charlie dabbed a wet washcloth on Mac's face and brushed her dark hair off her glistening forehead. "You're doing great."

A sense of longing tugged at Amanda's heart. Hopefully, this would be her and Tyler someday soon—married and having a little one of their own. After meeting at a holistic healthcare conference, they'd dated long-distance before Tyler Kelly had moved to Maple Valley to live closer to her. But after five years of dating, he still hadn't proposed. She'd given him subtle hints, watching *Say Yes to the Dress* and stopping in jewelry stores to *browse*. But something was holding him back.

Maybe he was waiting for this weekend.

She glanced up at the clock. Another midwife at the birth center was scheduled to take over for her in thirty minutes. Excitement bubbled in her chest. In just a few hours, she'd be on a plane with Tyler, replacing Iowa cornfields for Florida palm trees. They'd planned a short, relaxing trip for Labor Day weekend. And a great start to her vacation would be delivering Mac and Charlie's baby.

She checked the fetal monitor again. The heart rate had dropped to ninety beats per minute. Adrenaline coursed through her veins, fueling her with a sudden surge of anxiety. She asked Mac to change positions to see if it would make a difference.

It didn't.

Usually, she'd encourage her patients to listen to their bodies instead of telling them what to do, but Emma might have stopped breathing. "There's no time to rest. Push."

Mac looked at Charlie and blinked back tears. She hunched forward, letting a loud scream escape through her clenched teeth.

Emma's head moved down a little farther but not much.

A knot formed in Amanda's stomach. If Mac couldn't push her daughter out soon, she would have to be rushed to Furnam Hospital thirty minutes away from Maple Valley. The birth center didn't have the tools or staff to perform a C-section. "You need to get Emma out now," she said in an urgent tone.

Mac beared down as tears streamed down her flushed face.

Emma's head slid out of the birth canal with the umbilical cord wrapped around her tiny neck.

Amanda's heart thudded hard and fast against her chest. Even though nuchal cords were fairly common, the appearance of a cord wrapped around a baby's neck heightened her blood pressure. Without wasting any time, she unwrapped the cord in one quick, fluid motion.

Mac pushed again. One of Emma's shoulders slid

out, then the other shoulder.

Amanda held on to Emma as the rest of her little body appeared. She held her breath, waiting to hear Emma's first, sweet cries, but the infant wasn't crying.

All of Amanda's muscles tensed at once. Blood pounded in her ears to the rhythmic racing of her heart.

The assistants in the room rushed into action. One of the assistants quickly cut the umbilical cord and took Emma from Amanda. The assistant suctioned Emma's mouth and nose, clearing out fluid before laying the baby on the bed next to Mac. Another assistant placed an oxygen mask over Emma's nose to help her breathe.

Amanda forced her gaze away from the baby and tuned out the frantic conversation around her. She needed to deliver the placenta and stitch Mac's tear. She worked on autopilot, still waiting for a sign that the baby was okay.

Finally, a faint cry filled the room.

The tension in Amanda's shoulders lifted slightly. At least Emma was breathing. But why wasn't her cry stronger?

The assistants worked on Emma for several more minutes before one of their voices rose above the others. "Emma's oxygen level is alarmingly low."

Amanda stopped stitching and looked up. "Then we need to fly Emma to the NICU at Furnam Hospital."

Mac's eyes widened, her expression panicked as she

looked at Charlie, then Amanda. Her lips quivered. "Is Emma okay?"

Amanda gave Mac a weak smile. "Try not to worry. Emma is in good hands." Even to her own ears, she knew her response sucked. But she wouldn't make promises she couldn't keep.

IN THE BIRTH center's locker room, Amanda shimmied out of her dirty scrubs into yoga pants and a T-shirt with her favorite quote scrolled across the front: *Be the energy you want to attract.* At the sink, she washed her face, then tossed her hair into a messy ponytail. For a brief moment, she considered putting on makeup, but after dating Tyler for five years, she felt comfortable not getting all dolled up for him.

And she didn't feel like it anyway. Not with the uncertainty of Emma's condition weighing on her mind.

Over the last few years, she'd seen and delivered multiple babies who needed to go to the NICU. Many babies had been born with nuchal cords, like Emma, and most often those babies were just fine. Some had swallowed meconium or too much amniotic fluid and needed a few hours to recover. Other infants had been born early and needed the extra care.

But she'd also seen rare cases when infants were born

with life-threatening conditions. Hopefully, that wasn't the case for Emma and she wouldn't have to stay at the hospital for long.

Instinctively, Amanda clutched the locket at the base of her neck. She'd prefer not to remember the last time she'd visited Furnam Hospital.

Her phone vibrated on the counter. *Probably Tyler, wondering where I am.* He was supposed to pick her up and drive them to the airport. She glanced at her phone, seeing a message from Dad instead. *Have fun this weekend. Call me if you get something special.* Surprisingly, Mr. I-don't-understand-technology had added a winking emoji.

She rolled her eyes but smiled in spite of herself. So Dad wondered if this trip would end in an engagement, just like she did. Tyler had the whole trip planned—surfboard lessons at Cocoa Beach, a day at Epcot, and dinner reservations at the Rainforest Cafe. It would be the perfect trip for a proposal.

Slipping into a light jacket, she grabbed her duffel bag and walked quickly through the clinic. She dashed out into the night, scanning the brightly lit parking lot. Tyler's car wasn't here.

She chewed on her thumbnail. Tyler was never late. Usually, he liked to arrive early anywhere he went. Hopefully, nothing bad had happened, like a car accident or a … She stopped her thoughts from turning into worries. *Think positively.* Maybe a patient had shown up at Cory's Chiropractic, needing a last-minute adjustment. That seemed like a practical reason to be late. But even if that was the case, he could have at least texted her.

Amanda paced back and forth on the sidewalk. Her calves ached from Mac's long labor, but she couldn't sit still. If Tyler didn't get here soon, they would miss their flight.

A few minutes later, Tyler's Mercedes pulled into the parking lot at a leisurely pace and idled in front of the curb.

She flung open the passenger door. "Where—"

Tyler glanced in her direction and pointed to his cell phone. He lifted his pointer finger, signaling for her to wait.

Amanda tossed her duffel bag in the back and slid into the passenger seat. Who was he talking to? Based on his appearance, it didn't look like an easy conversation. His dark-blond hair looked slightly disheveled as if he'd been running his hands through it, and the sleeves of his dress shirt were haphazardly rolled up to his elbows.

Tyler spoke into the phone. "I'll be there tomorrow morning. Bye, Dad." He slipped his phone into the pocket of his dress pants and unbuttoned the top of his shirt, airing it out. "I have bad news."

"I take it we aren't going to Florida?"

"My dad needs me back in Chicago. Two of his chiropractors are sick with the flu. He's completely booked on Saturday, so he needs me to fill in. I'm so sorry."

Her dull headache turned into a throbbing pulse. She grabbed a bottle of peppermint oil from her purse and rubbed a little onto each of her temples as she contemplated what to say. "We've had this trip planned for months. You couldn't tell him 'no'?"

"I won't do that to my dad."

Amanda slumped back against her seat, fighting off disappointment, and losing the battle. "But you have no problem doing it to me." So much for being *the energy you want to attract*. But she couldn't help it. No romantic vacation. No secretly planned proposal. Her disappointment quickly escalated to frustration.

Tyler stared at the dashboard, his dark blue eyes unable to meet her gaze. He lowered his chin to his chest. "Honestly, I wasn't looking forward to this trip."

What? She froze for a moment, almost letting go of the bottle of peppermint oil as she waited for him to explain.

"Your dad left me a voicemail last night. He asked if I was going to propose to you on our trip."

"Seriously?" Leave it to Dad to meddle with her love life. Even though she was twenty-eight, he didn't know when to butt out. He'd done everything from reading her texts as a teenager, to following her on a first date, and now badgering her and Tyler about getting engaged.

"I didn't call him back. I didn't know what to say." Tyler unrolled his sleeves to button the cuffs. "Everyone is always putting pressure on us to get married, especially your dad. And lately, you've been watching all those wedding dress shows and looking at rings ..."

She frowned. So he had noticed after all.

"I wasn't planning on proposing during this trip, and after I heard your dad's voicemail, I figured you might have the same expectations. By the end of the weekend, you'd only be upset with me." Tyler ran a hand over his clean-shaven face. "I'm not ready to get married—you know what happened to my parents. They got married too quickly, hated each other for it, and then got divorced. I don't want that to be us."

His words knocked the wind out of her. How was she supposed to respond? Reassure him that it was okay? That her feelings weren't hurt? But none of that would be truthful. "It's not like we just met and we're rushing into an engagement."

He tugged at his tie and loosened the knot. Turning toward her, his lips formed a thin line and his Adam's apple bobbed up and down. "I think we should take a break."

She tightened her grip on the bottle of oil, then tossed it into her purse. No way had she heard him correctly. They were supposed to get married, start a family, and raise their kids in Maple Valley. Maybe not as quickly as she'd hoped, but she'd been willing to wait.

He reached for her hand, lacing his fingers between hers. "A break will give us time to think about what we want from this relationship."

"I already know what I want," she said quietly.

"I never intended to hurt you."

Amanda pulled her hand out of his grasp. "If you don't know what you want by now, then we aren't taking break." Anger slashed through the initial shock, shaking her to the core. "We're done."

She grabbed her duffel bag, flung open the door, and strode across the parking lot to her car without looking back. How could she have been so wrong about Tyler? He'd wanted a break when she'd been ready to commit to him forever.

About the Author

Crystal lives in Iowa with her husband and three growing children. She's a stay-at-home mom with a heart for people. She loves getting to know them, writing about them, and inventing them. When she's not hanging out with the hero and heroine in her latest book, she loves to dance awkwardly, watch reality TV, and visit real locations from her favorite books.

You can learn more about Crystal at her website www.crystaljoybooks.com.

Made in the USA
Monee, IL
05 December 2021

83708997R00166